T0346325

A Spy in Casablanca

A Spy in Casablanca

A Riley Fitzhugh Novel

Terry Mort

McBooks
Press

Essex, Connecticut

McBooks
Press

An imprint of Globe Pequot, the trade division of The Rowman & Littlefield Publishing Group, Inc.
4501 Forbes Blvd., Ste. 200
Lanham, MD 20706
www.rowman.com

Distributed by NATIONAL BOOK NETWORK

British Library Cataloguing in Publication Information available

Library of Congress Cataloging-in-Publication Data available

ISBN 978-1-4930-5838-9 (cloth)
ISBN 978-1-4930-5839-6 (electronic)

♾™ The paper used in this publication meets the minimum requirements of American National
Standard for Information Sciences—Permanence of Paper for Printed Library Materials, ANSI/
NISO Z39.48-1992.

CHAPTER ONE

"Do you know the line 'Where ignorance is bliss, 'tis folly to be wise?'"

"No. Dr. Johnson, I presume," I said. I knew that Johnson was the source of many of Bunny's quotes.

"Good guess, but no. It was a poet called Thomas Gray."

"Good to know. And?"

"Do you see that distinguished-looking gentleman over there, standing by that stunning woman in the black dress?"

"The old boy with a beard next to the femme fatale, half his age?"

"Yes, if you want to put it that way."

"The lady is bliss, the old boy, ignorance?"

"A tableau. Side by side. Almost an allegory."

"Allegory. Was it Mrs. Malaprop who said the Nile River was full of dangerous allegories?"

"Yes, it was. Bravo, Riley, old boy. I'm glad to see that the navy has not interrupted your reading."

"Not for lack of trying. But actually it's the Germans who keep interrupting."

We were at a cocktail party at the US Embassy in London. And from what I could tell, everyone was having a very good time. No one seemed the least depressed or worried. I guess the Brits were all used to the war by now. They'd been at it three years. And I was very happy to be there. The Germans had stopped bombing London for the time being; I and my ship, nicknamed the USS *Nameless*, had made it to England, if only just barely, and I was in one piece. What's more, I had run into an old friend. In fact, two of them.

Bunny was one. The other was Martha. So there were a few things to be grateful for.

Bunny, also known as Dr. Dennis Finch-Hayden, was formerly professor of art history at UCLA. He was currently involved in the military intelligence business for the British government. He was a friend from the old days in California, which chronologically were not that long ago—only a couple of years, in fact—but now seemed as remote as the Gilded Age. In many ways, they *were* the gilded age, the Great Depression notwithstanding. In contrast to the present, in gloomy, shattered, blacked-out London, that faraway time of just a few years ago was Arcadia. Of course, it helped if you lived and worked in Hollywood, where really the only glimpse of the Depression was in a Steinbeck novel. The Skid Row bums who wandered the tucked-away slums of LA had always been there. There were just a few more of them. But by and large it was business as usual in Hollywood, regardless of what the newspapers and politicians said.

"I take it the lady in black is attached to the old buffer in white whiskers," I said, "and that you are somehow involved with her, and he is somehow oblivious."

"You have not lost your detective instincts. Yes. Hence the quote from Gray, although he didn't mean it quite the way I do. He wrote it while he was wistfully admiring the playing fields of Eton and reflecting that the young gentlemen little knew what lay in store for them later in life."

"The happy days of innocence?"

"Yes. But you understand, I apply it in a slightly different way."

"Sure. It reminds me of a favorite line of mine—what the eyes do not see, the heart does not feel."

"You are a romantic empiricist."

"If you say so."

"She is beautiful, isn't she?" He said this in the tones of an art lover and critic, a connoisseur of beauty, which of course he was, personally and professionally. "And despite her husband's elderly looks, he is very energetic and works late at his diplomatic chores. Well past seven in the evening."

"Convenient."

"Yes. Perfect for *cinq à sept*."

Cinq à sept, a French expression meaning literally "five to seven," was, to Bunny's way of thinking, among the highest expressions of French culture, on par with Impressionism or Flaubert, for it referred to the two hours a man could spend with his mistress, drinking champagne and making love, after which they both could go to their respective homes and families and face the evening with equanimity and perhaps a secret smile or two. Quite possibly, the spouse wasn't really so ignorant and had some notion of what was going on, but didn't much care, having outside interests of his own. Or her own. But that wasn't a requirement. A clueless spouse was just as good as a complacent one. Bunny's evenings *après sept* were especially agreeable, because when he went home, there was no one to ask where he'd been. He was a confirmed bachelor, and his house-keeper, Mrs. Keppel, was not the curious type. So Bunny's smiles didn't have to be discreet. He would go through his mail, change for dinner, and then go out with friends and practice being charming, although he didn't really need the practice. He had mastered the elements, which is why the hours of five to seven were so varied and enjoyable for him. The rest of the time he was a spy.

I once teasingly asked him if he ever intended to marry.

"Marry? Have you ever heard of the former prime minister called David Lloyd George?"

"Vaguely."

"He was once preparing for a conference in Paris and someone asked him if he intended to bring his wife along, and he said, 'Would you take a sandwich to a banquet?' I don't think much of his politics, but you have to admire his sense of the fitness of things."

So the answer was no.

"Of course, his ungallantry is mitigated because he was married to a woman who, when asked advice about conjugal matters, said, 'Just close your eyes and think of England.'"

"Really?"

"It may be apocryphal."

"What does he do?" I asked, gesturing toward the old boy in the whiskers.

"The husband, there? Free French. Works for de Gaulle. Helps him make an arrogant pest of himself, not that de Gaulle needs much help along those lines. It's his greatest talent. Some think it's his only talent. Other than being tall."

"What do you think?"

"Oh, I couldn't possibly comment." He paused as he considered me for a few seconds. "I hear you had a rough time coming over."

"The U-boats were waiting, as usual. And the Luftwaffe. Half the ships in our convoy were sunk. We took a bomb on the fantail. Lost some very good men." All of them were good men, actually, and I said so in each of the letters I had to write to their parents or wives.

"Dreadful."

"Yes."

"What's the status of your ship?"

"It'll be a while before the repairs are done. We need quite a bit of work, and the shipyards are full as it is. We're in the queue on the Clyde. But there's no telling how long we'll be there. If we could make it back to the States, it'd be different. But we'd never make it there in our condition." In fact, if we tried, we'd sink in the Irish Sea. We would have gone down on the way in, if we hadn't been taken in tow by a British seagoing tug, bless 'em.

"What are you going to do?"

"Not much I can do. Learn to like warm beer and tea. And wait."

"But not alone, I hope. I see you have brought some company tonight."

"Yes." He was gesturing toward Martha, the other friend I had run into.

"She's a journalist, I understand."

"Yes."

"Someone's wife, too, I believe."

"More or less. We're just friends. I met her in Cuba."

The business about being friends was only part of the truth, as Bunny knew very well. Bunny knew just about everything, it seemed. But he of all people was not going to judge a wartime affair. Or a peacetime affair, for that matter. Affairs were one of his many specialties. He was something of a specialist in specialties, and although that is a paradox, or something, it fit Bunny, who was himself something of a paradox and therefore perfectly suited for his current job. Besides, with the war on and so many men and women being sent here and there, so many wartime separations, London was rife with people looking for some temporary connection, some antidote to loneliness. Affairs were as common as the fog.

"Very stylish woman," he said, looking at Martha, admiringly. She was chatting with some American general, gathering material for an article, but now and then she glanced over and smiled. "Brings to mind the word 'lissome.'"

"Yes."

That wasn't the word she brought to my mind, but I understood what he meant. She was tall and blonde and moved elegantly, like an athlete. She had lost her deep Cuban tan in the last few weeks and months, but even so she looked like her natural milieu was the out of doors, not a smoky cocktail party in a room filled with people in various uniforms, military and diplomatic. She had long blonde hair down to her shoulders, and she was the kind of woman people said was beautiful, even though she wasn't, particularly—until you got to know her, that is, and especially if you got to know her, intimately. Then she was very beautiful. In Cuba she liked to sunbathe and swim naked, and that was when she looked the best of all. Or second best. The best was when she was lying in bed with her eyes half closed and a languid smile that suggested contentment. But not many people saw that.

"So you'll have company while you're waiting for your ship to be put back together."

"For a while, at least. Until she goes off on her next assignment. Or has to go back to Cuba."

"Any interest in some temporary work?"

"Me?"

"Yes."

"Doing what?"

"Oh, this and that. Here and there. I could arrange it, I think. It'd be better than sitting around waiting for the shipyard to put your ship to rights."

"It's worth thinking about."

"Good. I'll look into it." Knowing Bunny, he had already looked into it, whatever it was, and had already made preliminary arrangements for whatever he had in mind.

So that's how I got into the espionage business.

Chapter Two

"How bad was it, darling?"

We were in Martha's rooms at the Dorchester, on Park Lane. Of all the fancy London hotels, it was the drabbest on the outside, especially now, with the sandbags piled outside the main entrance and the windows taped or boarded. On its best day, it looked like a branch of the Bank of England or the Board of Trade. Now it didn't look even that good. But the rooms were still luxurious, if just a bit worn. Across the street, Hyde Park was decked out in its summer green, but there were barrage balloons hovering above the nannies pushing prams and the little girls in pony clubs, riding on Rotten Row. You couldn't forget the war, even on a sultry Saturday evening.

"It was pretty bad," I said.

We were lying in bed without our clothes, which is how I realized that she had lost her dark Cuban tan. I hadn't seen her in a while. The last time I had seen her like this was on a beach on the Caribbean side of Cuba. She was brown all over then. That had been a good day.

"If you don't want to talk about it, it's okay," she said.

"You have enough material to write about, as it is?"

"God, yes. There's nothing but material."

"In that case, let's skip it for the time being. Let's talk about the next few days. I have a week's leave."

"How lovely. Let's go somewhere romantic."

"Paris is out, I'm afraid. But I'm open to suggestions."

"I know! We'll go out to Stockbridge. It's a little village in the country, not too far, so petrol shouldn't be a problem. I can get a car.

There's a charming hotel there. Very cozy. Very eighteenth-century. We can fish during the day and make love at night and sleep late in the mornings and have breakfast in bed and dinners in the pub. Bangers and mash and pints of local beer. Yum."

"Fish?"

"Yes. It's brilliant fishing there. The Test River runs right through town. We'll hire a gillie and catch some trout."

"That'll be a new experience for me."

"Even better. I can teach you. We can rent tackle at the hotel. It will be fun. Ernest would be green with envy, not that I'll tell him. The Test is a world-famous trout stream." Ernest was her husband and a well-known aficionado of all things having to do with fishing.

"It sounds perfect."

It didn't really, not the fishing part, but I didn't want to spoil her mood. And besides, she might be right. I might like it, too. The fishing part, I mean. I knew I would like all the rest of it, and, after all, wanting perfection is the best way to ruin your appreciation of the good things of life. I think Voltaire said something along those lines, and he was right about that, at least. A Bollinger '41 might not be a Veuve Clicquot '26, but it is still champagne. And if I'm entirely honest with myself, I can't really tell much difference.

"What do you want to do now, darling?" she whispered.

"I have an idea."

"Oh. So I see. *Encore?* Well, you have been at sea for a long time, haven't you?"

"Yes. And away from you even longer."

"I'm glad. Not about the separation. But about the reunion. Do you still like me even though my tan has faded?"

"Looking for a compliment?"

"Yes, of course."

"Well, then—*If ever any beauty I did see, which I desired, and got, 'twas but a dream of thee.*"

She looked at me for a moment, dropping all suggestion of flirtation.

"Are you serious?"

"Yes. In this case."

"That's a line from John Donne, isn't it? I think so."

"Yes."

"My God. I'd almost forgotten what a romantic you are."

"Someone has to be."

"You spoil me for the real world, you know."

"At your service, madame."

During this last Atlantic crossing, while we were shepherding the slow-moving convoy and when we were in the mid-Atlantic, and not yet into the danger zone of the Western Approaches, there was a lot of time to read, and I read most of John Donne. Not his sermons, but all the poems. He had a lot of good lines. That doesn't mean I didn't mean what I said to Martha. It just means Donne had a lot of good lines.

He also wrote *No man is an island*. I couldn't agree with him about that. *No man is an island?* Really? Once the Germans started their relentless attacks on our convoy, there were plenty of men left isolated and adrift, bobbing in the swells, pathetic specks we didn't dare to stop and rescue because of the U-boats below and the Luftwaffe bombers overhead. The best we could do was try not to run them down as we zigzagged at flank speed to avoid the bombs and torpedoes and the burning oil and smoking cargos. Those men blown into the water when their vessels sank sure looked like little islands, some waving to us to come back, others exhausted, oil-soaked, helpless, and resigned. They were alone in their fate, as forlorn as any useless speck of coral in the midst of nothing.

Of course, islands don't sink and drown, so in that sense, men aren't islands. But I don't think that's what Donne meant when he wrote that poem. I think he was talking about the brotherhood of man, or some such happy horseshit. Frankly, I couldn't see it.

And I remembered that Martha's husband had borrowed that poem for the epigraph of a book. I wondered if he really believed it. I don't think so. I knew him. Not that I wanted to think much about him—not while I was lying naked next to his naked wife.

"Speaking of John Donne," I said, "there's another pretty line that seems appropriate. But I'll save it for the morning."

"I'll bet I know. *And now good-morrow to our waking souls.* Is that it?"

"Nicely done. But you've ruined the surprise. I forgot that you went to Bryn Mawr."

"Only for three years. So you can tell me again in the morning. I promise I'll forget it tonight, if you give me something to take my mind off it."

"As I said, I am at your service."

"And I, my darling, am at yours."

"Well, then, *Where can we find two better hemispheres?*"

"God. I'm ruined. But, darling, let me ask you something. Are you sure I don't need a pillow under my ass?"

"I told you months ago in Cuba that that was nonsense."

"I was just wondering. I may have lost a few pounds, since I've been here. The food is bad for the figure."

"The only thing you've lost is your tan."

"I'm glad you think so. Now will you please do to me whatever you want to do?"

"How about if I do whatever you'd like me to do?"

"Mmm. I'll bet they're the same things."

I don't know who told her that business about the pillow. I could guess, but I wasn't sure. But whoever said it had hurt her, and it was unfair, because I wasn't lying when I said she didn't need one. She really didn't. But even if she did, it wasn't the kind of thing you'd say, if you cared about her. Or even if you didn't.

Chapter Three

It was Saturday. It was the last day of our week in the country, and it had turned out even better than expected. The weather cooperated. The days were sunny and mild and the evenings were cool in our rooms at the Grosvenor Hotel, a comfortable and venerable fishing hotel on the high street in the village of Stockbridge. The hotel owned a stretch of the Test River and let us fish there under the watchful eye of the local gillie, or guide. He was named William Sutcliffe, better known as Sunny Bill, because of his perpetual scowl and all around disapproval of anything not having to do with angling specifically, or country life and pastimes, generally. Hip boots were his footwear of choice, and every day he wore the same shapeless tweed jacket, green shirt, and brown knit tie. A tweed hat completed the outfit. And of course he had a very red face. His black Labrador, Jim, went with him everywhere, including the pubs.

"His full name is Lord Jim, after the book," said Bill. "But he's not a toff. Goes by plain old Jim."

"A dog of the people?"

"Up to a point, missy. Up to a point."

Martha already knew many of the secrets of fly fishing, and between her and Sunny Bill, I learned well enough to have a good time and understand why people liked the sport. Although of course to Sunny Bill it was much more important than any mere sport, and I knew better than to use that word about it in his presence. We caught a few fish to have for dinner at the hotel, but most of the time we'd let them go back into the river, much to Sunny Bill's disgust.

"You're teaching the buggers not to take the fly," he said.

"Come on, Bill, darling," said Martha. "They're not that smart."

"That's as much as you know, missy." But he said it with his version of a smile. He liked it when Martha called him "darling."

Bill also liked a pint or two after the day's fishing, and he and Jim always joined us in the hotel bar afterwards. Sometimes we'd sit in the garden behind the hotel. It was a perfect little garden surrounded by an ancient brick wall that was festooned with ivy and hollyhocks. At least, I think they were hollyhocks.

One late afternoon, while the three of us were sitting at a table there, we were joined by a young man with a friendly English face and pink complexion. He asked us, rather shyly, if he might join us. He knew Sunny Bill from before, so he assumed Martha and I must be all right, if Bill was willing to associate with us. He sat down and Martha asked his name, but he didn't respond for a second. I thought he might be distracted by looking at her, for the week of sunshine had brought back some of the color in her face. And our nights together had erased the traces of tiny frown lines. Mine, too. But it wasn't that.

"I'm sorry," he said, his voice raised. "I've gone a little deaf."

We must have seemed surprised that one so young had already lost his hearing.

"The kites are terribly noisy," he said, by way of explanation.

"Allister is in the RAF," said Bill, with a trace of pride. "Local lad makes good. Flies Spitfires, you know."

So here was one of Churchill's Few, one of the pilots who won the Battle of Britain in the air. He barely looked old enough to drive. His shyness around Martha made him seem even younger than that.

We exchanged stories for a while and then the boy pilot and Sunny Bill left for their homes, and Martha and I walked slowly down the village high street to the bridge over the river, and from there we walked along the riverbank until we came to a secluded spot we had found before while fishing, and we sat down in the grass.

"Do you remember that time in Cuba when I said we should be careful not to fall in love?" she said, after we had sat there a while, not saying anything.

"Yes, of course."

"And almost immediately afterwards I said I was in love with you?"

"You don't have to ask."

"No, I guess not. I'm sorry. And that's when you told me you felt the same . . . that you were in love with me."

"Yes."

"Is it still true, do you think? For both us?"

"I don't have to think about it."

"No. That's better. Better not to think. Not in this dreadful time. But it's hard not to, being out here in the country, where everything seems so peaceful and the awful war seems so far away, and there's just the two of us. You can almost start to believe that there's a future. Oh, dear. Am I starting to think in clichés?"

"No. I know what you mean."

I didn't say anything else. There was really nothing to say. I knew what was coming next. We had played this scene before.

"But it's hopeless, isn't it?" she said.

"Pretty much."

It was not hopeless because she was married. That was not going to last much longer, regardless of what happened or didn't happen between us. It was more the war and the long separations and the need to do the jobs we had asked for and still wanted to do. Yes, it was the war. And the fact of the war was too big to be a cliché.

"How sad."

"When do you leave?" I said.

"In another week or so. I'm not sure. But pretty soon."

"Where to this time?"

"Home, I'm afraid. The *Collier's* assignment is finished for the time being. There's only so much expense money available, and I don't want to wear out my welcome there. It's going to be a long war. I'll want more assignments. When do you go back to your ship?"

"In a few days. I'm having lunch with Bunny on Monday. He's got some sort of scheme up his sleeve. That may change things, somehow. I wouldn't be at all surprised if there weren't some new orders for me, waiting."

"Maybe they'll send you back to Cuba. Or Key West."

"Would you like that?"

"You know I would. Though it would complicate things, terribly."

"Well, I don't think it's likely. What are you going to do about the complications that are already there?"

"You mean Ernest? I don't know. I know it can't go on much longer. He wants me there to play Lady of the Manor. That won't work. I'm a writer, not a wife."

"I suppose it's theoretically possible to be both." Not in her case, though. I knew that.

"That's like saying that some animals mate for life, but when you look around to find some examples, all you can come up with is penguins and geese. Everyone and everything else is some version of Henry the Eighth or The Wife of Bath."

"And besides," I said, "how do we really know that geese and penguins mate for life? They all look alike. They could be fooling around, and the silly scientists who're watching them wouldn't know the difference."

"That's an old joke, darling."

"Yes. But a good one."

"You know, I think if I could get Ernest pried out of Cuba and over here to cover the real world and the war, we might be able to stand each other for a little while longer. But not much. And you know all about that."

"Not all. But I do know all I want to know."

"Yes. Much better that way. It's my problem, and what's happened between us is not the cause of it, in case you're wondering."

"Just a symptom?"

"Not that either. What you and I have is something apart from all that, something that lives and stays in our parallel world. Remember?"

"Yes."

I didn't really believe in what she called our parallel world. But if it made her feel better about things, I didn't mind going along with it. It was completely inconsistent with our knowledge that things were hopeless, but it was a pleasant fiction of permanence, with no harm in it, that I could see. Besides, she knew it was a fiction, too. Nobody believed in permanence these days. Everyone knew Heraclitus was right about reality. The war had just made it more obvious. More impossible to ignore.

"You know Eliot said mankind cannot stand too much reality," she said. "Yet here it is, staring us in the face."

"Eliot, the doorman at the Dorchester?"

"No. The other one. The make-believe Englishman. Shame on you . . . you who are such a fount of poetic quotes."

"My inventory is limited to poets who say beautiful things that I can repeat to beautiful women. I try to avoid dreariness."

"That I can believe, darling."

The crickets were starting to sing, and we could hear the gentle splashes of trout rising to take the mayflies off the smooth surface of the river. Now and then a pheasant would squawk, and we could hear the ever-present sound of the river gliding through the sedge on either bank. On the opposite bank we could see the willow branches moving gently as breeze passed through them.

"The wind in the willows," she said. "Do you know that book?"

"Yes. Bunny recommended it to me."

"Talk about a world apart. Another reality. So sweet."

"Yes. That's why I joined the navy—*Believe me, my young friend, there is nothing—absolutely nothing—half so much worth doing as simply messing about in boats. Simply messing.*"

"Nicely done. Is that really why you joined?"

"No. But it makes a good story."

She rolled on her side and looked at me.

"It's almost dark," she said. "I love this time of day. Do you think it's private enough here for us to make love? I'd like to have a memory of making love along this river. Then we'd always have it."

"It's dark enough. Besides, if we get caught, what are they going to do? Send us home as undesirable aliens?"

"I feel awfully passionate, just now. You can probably see the heat waves. I suppose by now you know me too well to be shocked. I didn't used to get this way, you know. I didn't used to like sex. It was just something you did to get it out of the way, so you could move on to things that matter. And I'm afraid when I leave, that old way of thinking is going to come back. But not tonight—not right now, God knows."

"If you're giving me the credit, I accept."

"Well, you get some of it, that's for sure. But you know, I'm also feeling pretty damned blue, even now, at this moment, even though things are so lovely. Maybe because they are."

"That's natural. So do I. *Aye, in the very temple of delight, veiled melancholy has her sovereign shrine.*"

"My God. You're a walking Bartlett's. Is that Donne, again?"

"Keats. 'Ode on Melancholy.'" I got through him, too, on the way over.

She sighed, melodramatically, ironically, sincerely, and lovingly, all at the same time. That was the way she was, and if I was truly in love with her, and I pretty much was, then that was part of the reason—her combinations.

"I'm a lost woman. You've spoiled me, you know."

"I don't believe that for a second."

"No?" She grinned, lasciviously. "You're right. I'm a woman who's about to make passionate love in the soft grass along the river. *Splendor in the grass.* You see? You're not the only one who can quote poetry."

"You must have gone to Bryn Mawr."

"Yes, for three whole years." She stretched and sighed again. "Isn't this lovely? Isn't it romantic? Aren't the meadow wildflowers beautiful? Doesn't the evening air smell good? Won't it feel good on our bare skin? And will you give me a hand with my buttons, please, darling? I could do it, but I like it when you do."

CHAPTER FOUR

THE FOLLOWING MONDAY, BUNNY AND I WERE IN THE UPSTAIRS library of Bellamy's, Bunny's club on St. James's Street. We were having a drink in this most private of club rooms. Bunny was dressed in his usual Savile Row, blue pinstriped suit, white shirt, and blue-and-white Eton tie. He was tall, fortyish, beaky, and blue-eyed. His wheat-colored hair was slicked back in matinee-idol style. Women thought he was devastatingly handsome, as well as charming. To me, he looked like an elegant Ichabod Crane. We first met in LA when I was working on a possible forgery case—a Monet. Bunny was our expert art consultant. That was back in the recent past, when I was a private investigator.

"No one ever comes up to the library, except to take a nap," said Bunny. "It's ideal for confidential chats, as long as some old buffer's not snoring away in the corner."

That day the room was empty except for the two of us.

"What do you know about Casablanca?" said Bunny.

"Casablanca? I know it's in production."

"Eh?"

"Our buddy Hobey wrote me about it. He tried to get hired to write the script, but they got someone else. A committee of some-ones. The story of his life, more or less. I imagine they've already started shooting."

Hobey Baker was a mutual friend from the Hollywood days, a formerly famous writer trying to repair his fortunes in the movie business and just barely getting by.

"Oh. I see. Well, too bad for Hobey, of course. But I wasn't talking about a movie. I was talking about the actual place. I assume you've heard of it."

"City in North Africa. Morocco. A French colony."

"Bravo. Actually, Morocco's a French protectorate. This is what's known as a euphemism."

"So it's a colony."

"You say potatoes and I say potahtoes. Ah . . . your security clearance is Top Secret, isn't it?"

"I'm sure you know that."

"Yes, well, one does check on these things, when necessary. Point is, I'm going to sketch a scenario, speaking of movies, and it needs to remain strictly between us. Even lovely blonde journalists with long legs are not to know of what I tell you. Agreed?"

"Of course. She's heading home soon anyway. But even if she weren't, I understand."

"Right. Then I'll put you in the picture and afterwards you can tell me if you want to stay there."

"You have a job offer?"

"Maybe. But it's only an idea at this stage."

Here it comes, I thought. As I suspected.

"Forgive me if I start at the beginning and tell you things you may already know, but it's best to have some notion of the full context."

"Of course."

He put his fingers together like the professor he used to be.

"So—when our erstwhile French friends surrendered, the Huns divided the country in two and let Marshal Pétain and his gang run the southern half from Vichy. They do so at the sufferance of the Huns and under the watchful eyes of the Gestapo, of course. But they do run things, including the army and navy. You have to understand that as long as Pétain and Vichy play ball, this arrangement suits the Germans nicely. They don't want to be bothered with administering the country or the colonies. It would take manpower and energy that they'd rather use elsewhere. They occupied all the French territory that they wanted, including Paris and the whole Atlantic coast, where they base the U-boats that caused you such headaches. But the levers of political administration are still French, meaning the police and security services, fire department, utilities— all of that. Even in the occupied sector this stuff is handled by the French."

"What about the French army?"

"Most of it is disarmed, disbanded and gone home. But there's enough left under the terms of the Armistice to keep a lid on things, especially in the colonies, where the natives might get restless, if they saw the lid slipping a bit."

"But they're under Vichy's command."

"Yes. The good news as far as Adolf is concerned is that quite a few of the boys in the Vichy government—and the occupied zone, too—are to some extent sympathetic to the Nazi ideology and think a crackdown on the leftist elements in France would be—and is—a good thing. Add to that, Pétain is unimpeachable, a hero, almost a mythical figure to the professional army. In the last war he defended Verdun, and everyone remembers. Plus, the old boy is a marshal of France. His word is law to most of the professional military, and if he says France is out of the war and they should cooperate with Adolf's boys, then they're out of the war and they'll cooperate with Adolf's boys. Pétain even came up with the word 'collaboration' to describe the way the French should deal with the Huns. He thinks he's saving what's left of France, and his officers think obeying him is a matter of professional honor. The professionals are still shattered psychologically by the collapse of the army. They'll cling to any fantasy or image of honor as a thin fig leaf to cover their drooping *amour-propre*. Telling themselves it's their sacred duty to obey Pétain is the fig leaf. In fairness, most of them really do believe it."

"What about de Gaulle? Where does he fit?"

"He doesn't. But you have to understand, he is a relative nobody in the army. What's more, he is a pain in the ass to anyone and everyone who knows him, friends and rivals alike. Worse still, he told us he could talk the French colonial forces in Dakar into surrendering and joining us in the great crusade, so we got together a commando force of our people and de Gaulle's so-called Free French and sailed down there, expecting a hero's welcome—or at the very least, a tepid sort of fight. But they gave him—and us—the bird and a bloody nose, and we sailed away looking damned foolish. De Gaulle most of all, in my view. He led the landing and was beaten off rather shamefully by French troops loyal to Vichy and Pétain. De Gaulle's even regarded as a traitor in some circles, because he's not falling in line with Pétain. He'd probably be in jail somewhere, if he weren't in England. He wants to fight on; Pétain says it's over. So it's over, as far as most of the French professional officers are concerned. Oh, we'll make use of de Gaulle to the extent that he can be useful—making radio broadcasts and so on. But he's no modern-day Jeanne d'Arc, despite what he thinks."

"What about the Resistance?"

"Mostly disorganized civilians. A lot of them are leftists who want to change the way France looks after the war. They want to get rid of the Germans, so that they can bring in the Russians, if not in fact, then in spirit. Other groups, who think like de Gaulle, have a different view of the present and the future, and all these various groups have only the shakiest working relationship. After the war, once the Allies have sent the Germans back to the hairy embraces of their Brunhildes, the French leftists and the Gaullists and Pétain's collaborationists will all be at each other's throats. That goes for the gangs in France *and* in the colonies.

"The thing to keep in mind is that the African colonies mirror the political and military situation in France. Opinion is divided, but power resides with the Vichyites. What's more, the last thing the French army in the colonies wants to do is antagonize their German overlords, because they need to keep the Arab population in check, and if the colonial army is diminished in either strength or prestige, the fear is the natives will notice."

"Sounds like a cage of parrots."

"Yes. Very apt. Because if you've ever seen a French general, he very much resembles a parrot—beautiful plumage, often with a large beak and a haughty demeanor that's totally out of touch with the abject reality of his situation—the unpleasant fact that he's in a cage. The same goes for the navy. Bloody-minded bastards, many of them. They don't really think they had much of a hand in the defeat, and their head man, Darlan, is solidly in bed with Vichy. Needless to say, the French navy doesn't care much for the English."

"Because of Mers-el-Kébir."

"Precisely. It still rankles."

"You can hardly blame them."

"No, in fairness, you can't. But it complicates things greatly."

Mers-el-Kébir was a French naval base in Algiers. When France surrendered in June of 1940, much of the French fleet was in Mers-el-Kébir, and Churchill and the general staff were terrified that the ships would fall into German hands, either voluntarily or by capture. If the Germans commandeered the French navy, the Med could well become an Axis lake. The Luftwaffe based in Italy made things hazardous enough already; the Italians had a useful navy, and the addition of French warships would make a disastrous combination. They would probably cut off the British lifeline to the Suez Canal. The British presence in tiny Malta would be impossible, and Gibraltar would most likely fall, perhaps even invaded by Hitler's chum, Franco. Therefore, the Mediterranean must remain under the control of the Royal Navy, but it would be a close-run thing even without the French warships. According to the terms of the Armistice with

Germany, the French navy was under the command of the Vichy government and had therefore promised to remain out of the war.

But those assurances were not enough for the Brits. The ships had to be neutralized—and not with some scrap of signed paper that could be torn up as easily as Hitler's promise not to attack Russia.

Churchill repeatedly asked the French to send their ships to the Western Hemisphere, preferably to their island of Martinique, where the Yanks could keep an eye on them. But the French refused. And so Churchill decided he had no choice and sent a task force to destroy the French ships in Mers-el-Kébir. After repeated warnings the British opened fire, sank a number of French ships lying at anchor, and killed almost thirteen hundred French sailors and marines, losing two men in the process. Vichy France broke off relations with Britain, and, as Bunny put it, with a certain understatement, the incident still rankled. It was only two years ago.

"Interestingly, since we're on the subject of Casablanca," said Bunny, "one new French battleship, the *Jean Bart*, was not in Mers-el-Kébir, but in Morocco, getting repairs. There she sits in the port of Casablanca."

He looked at me for a moment, smiling enigmatically. Was this the rat I had been smelling?

"I see," I said. "And I suppose you're going to ask me to lead a commando team in there and blow her up."

He looked at me, feigning astonishment.

"What a good idea! Do you think you can do it?"

"Not in a million years."

"I agree. And you'll be relieved to know that that's not the job I may be offering you. In fact, it never occurred to me."

"I'll bet."

"There's another layer to the story. Uncle Joe Stalin has been clamoring for us to open a second front to relieve some of the pressure on Russia. The Reds are taking a pasting, although the signs are the Huns may have stepped into the treacle here and there, and things could get sticky for them. Roosevelt and Churchill want to help out—not from any love of the Reds, but for fear the Huns might knock them out of the war and then turn their full attention on us. So a second front makes good strategic as well as political sense.

"But there is disagreement on just where to do this. Your people want to go across the Channel into France. As soon as possible, meaning this year. Next year at the latest, although waiting even that long won't suit Uncle Joe at all. Our chaps think invading France within a year even would be premature. We're not ready, and the last thing we want is to get bogged down in a bloody stalemate in the trenches, like the last war. There are far too many war memorials in Britain for anyone to want to do that again. You can see where this is going, I assume."

"Yes. North Africa will be the second front."

"In a nutshell, yes. The Germans are already there in Libya, threatening Egypt and Suez, so it makes sense to stop them by threatening their rear. The invasion should be a cakewalk, since if we hit the French colonies, they might not even resist. There's a chance that they will, but ideally the French army there will see the error of their Pétain-istic ways and throw in with us. That's the hope, anyway."

"Especially if the Yanks are leading the invasion parade, not the Brits."

"Ah, yes. Then, once we've jointly dealt with Rommel and the Afrika Korps, North Africa can become a staging area for an eventual invasion of Europe, probably into Southern France, or maybe Italy. Winston seems to think that Italy is what he calls the 'soft underbelly.' So strategically, it all makes a certain amount of sense."

"And what is this idea you have?"

"Well, it's simple really. You see, when France capitulated and established the new government in Vichy, the United States recognized the new arrangement, diplomatically. As a result you have active consulates in Morocco and Algeria. And the Consulate in Casablanca needs a new naval attaché, and I was thinking you might like the job—temporarily, of course, while you wait for your ship to be put back together."

"I see. How long would I be there? And what would I be doing?"

"It could be just a matter of a month or two. You see, there's a river we'd like to know a little more about. It's called the Sebou. It's north of Casablanca a bit, and toward the upper end of it, there's a French air base. Rather a good one. In fact, it's the only one in North Africa with concrete runways. We'd like to have it remain intact after we—meaning, you Yanks—land. It will be very useful in a number of ways. First, to gain control of the air and support the landings. We can fly planes in from Gibraltar, as well as those off any carriers you might bring along. And just as importantly, if the Jerries and the Spanish decide to attack Gibraltar, we'll need planes to support the defense."

"I get it. And concrete will support the heavies."

"That's it. The easiest way to take it is with an amphibious force. Much better than slogging overland through the desert."

"What about paratroops?"

"That's possible and under consideration. But for reasons I don't quite understand—possibly availability—they may not be an option. We have to plan for the alternative."

"An amphibious assault upriver."

"Yes. But we don't know if the river's navigable all the way. Rumor has it that it's a very tricky piece of water. And the airfield is very important to the overall attack, because you Yanks have only one attack aircraft carrier available for this operation. The others are in the Pacific—some, unfortunately, at the bottom of it. As a stopgap, we—meaning you—have converted some oilers to flattop aircraft carriers, with the emphasis being on the word 'carriers.'

Some of these vessels will be carrying army P-40s. These vessels will be able to launch aircraft—but not recover them. So once launched, the planes will need some place to land, refuel, and rearm."

"So you're saying the airfield is the key to the attack on Morocco."

"One of them, certainly. An important one. But as I said, we don't know if going up the river is feasible. However—if some enterprising naval attaché could find out whether an amphibious operation could work, it would make planning for the overall attack so much easier. We could send one of our chaps, perhaps, but the French don't seem to like us—they severed diplomatic relations after Mers-el-Kébir. They do seem to be fond of you Yanks, however. They don't realize that you all are just Englishmen gone bad."

"I see."

"Care to take a flutter?"

"Not especially."

"Really? I'm surprised." He didn't sound surprised. But then he never did. "I would have thought this sort of thing was right up your street. As I recall, you used to be a private investigator. In fact, that's one of the reasons you were thought of for this job."

I noticed that he used the passive voice—"were thought of"—as if this weren't his idea and suggestion.

"It really isn't that much that much different from sleuthing around in Hollywood."

"Casablanca isn't Hollywood."

"Isn't it? Really, my friend, there's not much to this. Fly in, have a look, fly back and rejoin your ship, and accept the thanks of two grateful nations."

"Easy for you to say. But you're overlooking a major problem. If I did this, it would require a set of formal orders, you know. I just can't go traipsing off to North Africa."

Bunny smiled and tapped his breast pocket.

"No trouble, there, old boy. It's a volunteer mission, of course, but I've taken the liberty of greasing the official skids just a bit."

It figured.

"I'm curious. Why are you involved? Why isn't one of our people making this contact? Someone from our naval intelligence, or OSS?"

"Well, dear boy, the OSS is in fact making the contact, because I've been seconded to your people. It's all in the interests of Anglo-American cooperation. In all fairness, the OSS is rather new at this espionage game, and we devious Brits have been at it for a few centuries now. And since this North Africa will be a joint operation, it was felt that someone with my knowledge of our former colonials, meaning you chaps, could be useful. After all, I lived in Hollywood for years."

"Don't your people know that Hollywood isn't really part of America? And in fact doesn't really exist at all?"

"No. They think it's a real place."

"So you are officially working for the OSS?"

"Temporarily, yes. And I have to say, I like your people very much—an interesting collection of warriors, scholars, and sophisticated men. But still largely babes in the espionage woods. I'll do my bit to help out. And we are offering you the chance to do the same while you are waiting around with nothing to do. But here's the thing you must understand above everything—the whole war effort, including our vital relationship with the Russians, depends on the success of this invasion, and the success of the invasion depends on you! Just like in the movies!"

"What? Are you serious?"

"Ha! Just kidding, old boy. If you get captured or killed, it won't make a damned bit of difference to the war. Not that we wouldn't miss you. But you know, you just may be able to help move things along a bit. Somebody's going to go in there and figure that river out. Why not you? After all, you don't really have anything else to do right now. Mrs. Hemingway is heading back to Cuba."

"Tell the truth, Bunny. Do I have any real choice in this?"

"Officially, yes, because it's a volunteer mission."

"And unofficially?"

"Not much. You know how these things work. You've been in the navy long enough by now."

"Yes, I know. In that case, what are my chances?"

"Of surviving? Quite good, really. Aside from the possibility of assassination by the Gestapo or the Vichy police, there's very little risk. After all, you'll be going in as a member of the officially recognized American Consulate. Getting into the country is no trouble at all."

"And getting out?"

"Slightly more complicated, but not much, assuming everything goes well. Legally speaking, the Vichy police could make trouble for you, but your diplomatic status makes it a little more difficult than, say, throwing a beggar in jail."

"What about when I'm skulking through the desert, like Lawrence of Arabia in a burnoose? That might raise some suspicions."

"Ah. Well, there's that possibility, of course. In that case, I suggest a fez rather than a burnoose. A flowing robe makes it harder to run. Which reminds me of a joke. A man meets another in the kasbah and says, 'I don't remember your name, but your fez is familiar.' Rather elderly, that joke, but I like it."

"Hilarious."

"And by the way, word has it that an old friend of ours is in town. In Casablanca, I mean. Amanda Billingsgate."

"Really? That's interesting." Yes. That was interesting.

"I thought you would think so."

"Who's she working for?"

"I'm not sure."

"Aren't you people supposed to know these things?"

"You would think so, wouldn't you? But this spy game is a game within a game. There are players who are supposed to be on the same side, but who keep their own counsel. Your people are the worst, I'm sorry to say. The FBI and army and naval intelligence are all closed shops. The OSS is the new boy and is regarded with suspicion and, sadly, lack of cooperation. We Brits had a similar problem, until Winston or someone in his government knocked everyone's heads together and told them to play together nicely. And it still doesn't work perfectly. Point being, Amanda could be working on the side of the angels without the other angels knowing about it. All the European countries, even including the neutrals and the ones Adolf conquered and occupied, have their own intelligence agencies. Some have escaped to Britain. Some are operating undercover at home. No one wears a name tag or a badge. Too bad, really. At least we'd know who the good guys are."

"How about the Russians? Could she be working for them?"

"Ah, well, that is certainly a possibility. Yes, I hadn't thought of that one."

"I'll bet."

"Well, if you did, there's a good chance you'd win."

Chapter Five

Two days later, I was at an air base outside of London, waiting to catch a flight to Gibraltar. From there I would hop across the Straits to Tangier, where I would meet with the head OSS man in the region. After that, I assumed I'd be off to Casablanca to take a look at a river in the desert.

Martha came to the air base to see me off. We were standing on the tarmac, beside my plane.

"Good-bye, darling," she said. There weren't any tears in her eyes, but her voice sounded strained. "I'll be leaving soon, too," she said. "I just got a call from a friend in the air corps. He's managed to get me a space on an army plane heading home."

"Is he in love with you, too?" I said. And I said it with a smile, so that she would take it as a compliment, which is how I meant it.

"Thank you for saying 'too.' I'll ask him and let you know. You will look after yourself, won't you?"

"Yes."

"That's a silly thing to say, isn't it."

"Maybe. But it's expected in scenes like this. And it's my turn to say the same thing to you."

"I will. Take care of myself, I mean. You know me. And assuming we don't get shot down, my biggest challenges, once I get home, will be boredom laced with domestic tension, at least until I can wangle another assignment. I'm stopping off in New York and maybe if I sit on someone's lap at *Collier's*, they'll think of something else for me. I'll write to you. Will you write to me?"

"Of course."

She had a private, personal post office box in Havana. I had sent letters there in the past. She sent her letters to me via the Fleet Post Office, and they eventually got to the ship. But for the next month or so, my address would be the US Consulate in Casablanca.

"I'm very much in love with you, you know," she said. "If anything, the week we've just had has made it worse."

"For me, too. And you know, of course, that I feel the same way."

"You're in love with me, too."

"Desperately," I said, smiling, to balance the melodrama.

" 'Desperately' is good," she said.

"Thank you."

"If I ever write this scene, I may use it."

"And when I read it, I'll remember."

"You'd better."

Then she smiled slightly and kissed me and turned around quickly and hurried to the cab that was waiting. And that was the end of it. Aside from the little jokes, it was a pretty typical wartime farewell scene. That was all right. There's not much room for originality in situations like this, so there's no need to wish for it.

Would I ever see her again? How the hell did I know. We had made no promises, other than to write and try not to get ourselves killed. But I hoped I would—see her again, I mean. Was I really in love with her? Yes, I was, although I'm not sure "desperately" was the best way to describe it. And I believed she meant what she said to me. We both knew ours was a far-above-average love affair. In peacetime, it might've had a chance of lasting for a while. But this was wartime, and things had a way of happening.

The plane was a Lancaster bomber that made a regular run to The Rock. We took off and swung well out into the Atlantic, beyond the range of Luftwaffe fighters, before turning and making a dash to the east and setting down nicely in Gibraltar.

The Brits welcomed me and gave me a room in the Royal Navy bachelor officers' quarters. I only had that evening to look around. But I didn't feel much like sightseeing. Most of the actual Rock was off limits, anyway, and I had no interest in seeing the Barbary apes. I agreed with Mark Twain when he said the Almighty must have designed humans because He was disappointed with the monkey. I knew some excellent specimens of humanity, but not all that many, and most of the rest of the species didn't impress me much. And I'm pretty sure they would return the compliment. So I certainly wasn't interested in looking at failed prototypes.

On the flight down to Gibraltar, I couldn't help thinking about Amanda Billingsgate and wondering if I'd run into her in Morocco. Casablanca was a pretty big town, but the foreign community tended to hang around the same places. At least, that's what Bunny had told me. Chances are, I would see her, unless for some reason she didn't want to be seen. That was a possibility. If she was up to some nefarious espionage business, she might not want to be seen by anyone from her past. But I hoped I would—see her again, I mean. Amanda and I had what's known as a history. And it was the good kind. She always reminded me somehow of butterscotch. It was mostly her coloring, and I wondered if she'd changed that. If she was involved in the spy business, it would have been the sensible thing to do. But it would be too bad.

I have to confess—I also wondered about having those pleasant thoughts and memories about Amanda. After all, it wasn't too many hours before that I'd said good-bye to Martha and also said some pretty serious things to her, and heard the same things from her. And that made me think that maybe Mark Twain had got the order of creation backwards, at least in some cases. But I dismissed that idea, as well as any budding feelings of guilt. You can't help what you think. That's why it's generally best not to do it, when complicated matters of the heart are concerned. Other times, of course, it's useful. Even necessary.

Besides, Bunny was the one who brought her up. Amanda, I mean. If he hadn't, she would have remained a name from recent history. If she had returned to my thoughts, it wasn't my fault. A rationalization? Maybe. But I could live with it. I did wonder if he had mentioned her just to sweeten the deal he was offering me. God knows there was very little sweetness about the rest of it. I had raised my hand and said yes, but at the moment I had a mild case of volunteer's remorse. That's normal, of course, but knowing that doesn't make it go away.

— ⁓ —

The next morning I hopped a ride with a Royal Navy patrol boat, and we headed across the Strait for Spanish Morocco and the city of Tangier. Morocco was theoretically ruled by a Muslim king, but in fact it was divided into two protectorates, which was the fig-leaf term for colonies. The northern portion along the coast was run by the Spanish, while the southern portion, which was far larger, belonged to France. Tangier was supposed to be an open city under the international agreements that set up this whole arrangement, but a couple of years ago, after winning his civil war, Franco decided to absorb the city, and so he was now running things in Tangier. The international community didn't say much about it, as far as I knew. All those diplomats sitting around long tables were used to making elaborate treaties that other diplomats and their bosses would ignore when it suited them. It was how things worked.

The boat ride was pleasant and the patrol craft was sleek and fast, and in a couple of hours I was in the capital of wartime espionage. Or at least, one of them.

There was a US sailor and a jeep waiting for me when I arrived in the very busy port. He came up and saluted smartly and said he'd come from the Consulate to pick me up and take me to Lieutenant Colonel William Eddy, who was the naval attaché in Tangier, and my contact in the OSS.

"What's your name, sailor?" I asked my driver, when we had settled my luggage and climbed into the open-air jeep.

"Davis, sir."

"How do you like being posted here?"

"Well, sir, it's one of the best places in the world, if you want a dose of the clap."

"Good to know."

It didn't take long to realize that Tangier was city that would depress all but the most optimistic missionary with the hopelessness of his task—assuming his task involved conversion and reformation and rejection of any and all sins, deadly and otherwise. In fact, missionary optimism alone wouldn't suffice. Blind innocence and a healthy dose of saintliness might make someone believe in the essential goodness of mankind, or even in the possibility of improvement. Anyone else would see clearly that the human race was a mess, and that Tangier had collected the sour cream of the crop.

Not that it wasn't interesting to me. Actually, I was expecting something along these lines, and I was not disappointed. First, there was the port itself, crammed with shipping from all over the world and loaded with cargo, some of it legitimate, some of it headed for illegal harbors. And, like any international port, the docks and adjacent streets were no places for your grandmother. But if you wanted a grandmother, there'd be a pimp who'd get you one and guarantee she was a virgin and had a clean certificate of health. She'd meet you near the end of the next alley and you shouldn't mind the merchant sailors you had to step over to get to her.

That was just for starters.

Away from the port and in the city, there were a couple of thousand desperate refugees from all across Europe, most of whom would do anything to find a way out of there, so that they could get to somewhere leading to anywhere else, as long as it was free from Franco's police, Nazis, and the local Gestapo thugs.

The refugees were milling around, desperately harried by local con artists who would sell them whatever they needed in terms of paperwork. Paperwork was easy to forge, and there was a willing market just waiting to be cheated. In the mix with these frightened Europeans were a few thousand Spanish communists and escapees from the Civil War. They hated Franco and his goons and were of course making plans and plots to get their revenge. The native Berber population, along with smatterings of other North African tribes, were the teeming majority, but they were also the indigenous underclass typical in any European colony. Their allegiance to their European masters was wavering, or, rather, nonexistent. They didn't care who won the war, because they only wanted their independence, and anyone who lied to them convincingly about helping them get it had a receptive audience. They disliked being shoved around by Franco's police and didn't like being thought of as virtually subhuman. It didn't seem unreasonable to me, but their European bosses didn't think they were ready to look after themselves, and told them so.

So, if you take all these incompatible peoples and cram them in a city of narrow streets and alleys that wind around dark and dirty neighborhoods with sinister-looking men and sinister-looking women all dressed in sinister-looking clothes tending sinister-looking urchins throwing stones at sinister dogs, all of them with that "lean and hungry look," and you set all these characters lurking in the dirty, littered stinking neighborhoods, you would have the essence, and I do mean *essence*, in the Chanel sense of the word, of Tangier.

True, the main part of the city was almost recognizable as a civilized place, with hotels and government buildings here and there and more bars and nightclubs than you could count in an evening's wanderings. The minarets where they called the faithful every few hours gave the place an Arabian nights atmosphere. But on balance the city was a steaming pile of depressing humanity that made you wonder about a lot of things, metaphysical and otherwise.

There is the kind of person who revels in all of this and thinks it's colorful, which it is, and also thinks its diversity is enchanting. I didn't fall in that particular camp. What was it Martha had said? Mankind cannot stand too much reality? Well, here it was staring me in the face. I could stand it. But as I surveyed the scene, I thought fondly of the swimming pool around the Garden of Allah Hotel— the Hollywood pleasure dome and fraternity house where I used to live—and of the starlets who came there in the fragrant evenings to swim naked, while the various degenerate writers and actors sipped gin and tonics and enjoyed the spectacle and hoped that Kismet would deliver one or more of these houris to their room. I much preferred those ersatz Arabian nights to this real thing. Too bad. Hollywood was a long way away. I had joked to Bunny that it didn't really exist, and from the perspective of faraway Tangier, it was easy to believe that.

We drove through the narrow, littered streets, and in one alley a gang of kids, all about eight years old on average, gathered and followed along behind us, shouting something. Davis reached in his pocket and pulled out a pack of Lucky Strikes and tossed them over his shoulder. The pack of kids fell on the cigarettes like sharks on a dead whale. "They start smoking early here," he said. "Luckies are their favorite. 'LSMFT—Lucky Strike means fine tobacco.'"

I thought the advertising agency that had dreamed up that slogan would be proud to know it was being quoted in faraway Tangier.

Then we pulled out on the wide boulevards of the main city. We weren't headed for the official US offices, though.

"Colonel Eddy wants to meet you at his villa outside of town, sir," said Davis. "That's about the only place you can be fairly sure of having a private conversation. He also has rooms at the El Minzah Hotel in town, but those rooms are bugged, and every maid and waiter is being paid by somebody, maybe by more than one somebody, to report whatever they hear and collect any scrap of paper they can lift from the wastebaskets. The Consulate and all our offices are bugged. Even the head. Phones, too. It's a good way to pass along phony information to the Krauts and Eyeties and the matadors."

It took about half an hour to get to Eddy's villa in the country. When we left the city and went out into the countryside, it looked a lot like Southern California. The weather was sunny, not surprisingly, and the dry desert air also reminded me of California. It was a welcome change after my last year, stationed in Key West and Havana, where the air was half liquid most of the time. And shepherding slow convoys across the Atlantic was an exercise in weeks of nothing but the damp and mold. So it was good to feel dry all over, even if you paid for it by being in North Africa.

The villa was on a small hill, and you could see the Atlantic in the distance. On a very clear day you could make out the tip of the Rock of Gibraltar across the Strait. The house was large and white, of course, and there was a small garden and patio on the side. Orange trees and cactus were mixed with the flowers.

"Where's all the sand, Davis? I thought we were supposed to be in the desert."

"Go a little ways east, Lieutenant. Climb over those Atlas Mountains there and look toward Egypt; you'll have all the sand you want for as far as you can see. That's the Sahara, and thank God it's on the other side of the mountains."

"Well, the colonel's villa is in a pretty spot," I said, as we pulled into the well-maintained gravel driveway.

"Being a colonel's a good thing."

"How about being a seaman, first class?"

"Less good, but still better than being any of these beggars in this godforsaken part of the world."

Frankly, it didn't seem that godforsaken, now that we were out of the teeming city.

Colonel Eddy had seen us driving up and was on the patio when we arrived. I could see that he walked with a pretty severe limp and used a cane.

I got out of the jeep and waved. Neither one of us was wearing a uniform so there was no saluting required.

"I'll wait for you, sir," said Davis. "I imagine you'll be going to the hotel, when you're finished with the colonel."

"The hotel that's bugged?"

"They all are, sir, but you'll be going to the El Minzah. It's the best in the city. Highest-quality bugs."

"It's good to be a naval attaché."

"That's the truth, sir."

I walked over to the patio and introduced myself to Colonel Eddy.

"Good to meet you," he said with a friendly smile. "Welcome aboard." He turned to Davis. "Has the drip cleared up, Davis?"

"Almost, sir."

"Good. Let that be a lesson to you."

"I've learned it, sir."

"Go around to the kitchen and get a beer. Mr. Fitzhugh and I will need about an hour, then you can take him back to town."

"Aye, aye, sir."

Eddy laughed and said to me, "The only thing Davis has learned is not to go back to that same house. Let's sit on the patio and have a drink. Gin and tonic suit you?"

"Yes, sir."

We sat down at a table under an orange tree and a navy steward took the drinks order.

Eddy looked like a movie extra, but not the handsome kind—more like the kind who plays the camp cook on a cattle drive or a rugged sergeant major in the cavalry. Everything about him seemed to be thickset, including his face. But there was no fat on him. There was a trace of bulldog, too, as though he were a distant, younger cousin of Churchill.

"The only people working here are sailors and marines," he said. "No locals or Europeans. Frankly, you can't trust anyone you're not absolutely sure of. That's the first lesson to learn about this part of the world. That sounds like something out of *The Boys' Book of Adventure*, but it's the unvarnished truth."

"Davis was telling me that all the offices are bugged."

"It's true. And we're followed wherever we go. I know for a fact that there are at least fifty-five Gestapo agents in the city, alone. Those are the ones we know about and have pictures of. Who knows how many more there are? The only business we conduct at our offices is meaningless busywork or counterintelligence stuff—passing phony information through the thin walls or over the telephone. We do the important business out here. Maybe you noticed the marine sentries arranged around? Nobody gets in here."

"I saw a few."

"You didn't see them all. Do you carry a handgun?"

"No, sir. Should I?"

"Never hurts. You can draw one from the Consulate. You'll have to sign for it and turn it in when you leave. You know how that works."

"Yes, sir." I wouldn't need to draw one. I had my .38 in my luggage.

"What do you think of the country so far?"

"Interesting."

"Ha! That's what people say about modern art. Well, if you stay here long enough you may get to the point where you appreciate it. You know what the English say about India—'You hate it for the first six months you're there and love it for the rest of your life.' It's the same here. For some."

"I figure to be out of here before six months, Colonel."

"One way or the other, eh? I understand. The country takes some getting used to, but I like it, and I like the people very much. Of course, I was born in the Middle East. My folks were missionaries. So I grew up speaking Arabic alongside English. Arabic's an interesting language. Very difficult, but not if you take to it as a kid. Lots of different dialects, of course, but they all can understand each other pretty well. And the calligraphy is exquisite. How's your French?"

"I can order a beer."

"Well, that should be good enough. Most people you'll need to deal with can get by in English. I figure they thought of that when they gave you this job. So, speaking of that—what have they told about your mission?"

"Well, sir, not really all that much. They want to know if the Sebou River north of Casablanca is navigable. They're pretty much leaving it up to me to figure it out."

"That's because you've been lent to the OSS. That's how we do business. Figuring it out as we go along. Leaves lots of room for initiative and screwups. Even a touch of farce now and then. How's our friend Bunny Finch-Hayden?"

"Very well. He sends his regards."

"Good fellow. I met him when I was in London this last trip. You'd think only the English would saddle a kid with that nickname, but Edmund Wilson is called that, too. Know of him?"

"Only by reputation."

"Bit of a stuffed shirt, despite being a Princeton man." Our drinks arrived. "Well, cheers—and here's to the success of your mission."

Bunny had briefed me about Colonel Eddy. He was an altogether remarkable man. Born in Lebanon to Presbyterian missionaries, he was sent back to the United States for his education. After graduating from Princeton in 1917, he joined the marines and was wounded in France. Shortly afterwards he was caught in the Spanish flu epidemic that caused some severe infections that required surgery, damaging his hip joint so badly that he walked with a limp from then on.

When the war was over he went back to Princeton and got his PhD in English, taught at Dartmouth College for a while, and then became president of Hobart College. When the current war broke out, he rejoined the marines and then found his way into the fledging OSS, which resulted in his assignment as naval attaché in Morocco. He spoke a couple of other languages, in addition to Arabic, and had written his doctoral dissertation on satire in *Gulliver's Travels*. So he had a healthy taste for irony and humor of all varieties, mixed with a missionary son's sense of duty and a marine's sense of honor and devotion to one's country. He had a loving wife and family back home. He was friendly, even gregarious, and could get along with almost anyone, but he did not suffer fools at all. He was exactly the way you'd design a warrior-diplomat-spy, if you knew what you were doing.

"What were you doing before you got lassoed into this business?"

"I was the executive officer on the *PC-475*," I said. "We were escorting a convoy to England and got hit pretty hard by a bomb from a Heinkel 111. The ship's scheduled for repairs at the Clyde River shipyard, and it'll take a while to put her back together. So Bunny thought I might like a temporary assignment."

"What did you do before the war?"

"I was a private investigator in Los Angeles. That's how I got to know Bunny."

"Yes, he told me he taught at UCLA."

I was glad he didn't smile or make a joke about trench coats, when I told him about being a PI. A lot of people seemed to think it was funny, somehow. He didn't. I guess it was no more unusual for a former private dick to be in this spy business than a former college professor. As I was to learn, the unusual was common in the OSS.

"How much do you know about Operation Torch?" he said.

"Not much, sir. What little I know about anything is pretty much confined to questions about the Sebou River. Planners want to know if a supply vessel could get upstream as far as the airport. Twelve miles or thereabouts. Why they want to know it is pretty clear, but I don't know much more than that. Not much about the bigger picture."

"Better that way, I think. That way, if you're captured and questioned, you won't be able to tell them anything they don't already suspect." He smiled. It was not exactly a grin, but close. "The truth is, if they did capture and interrogate you, they'd probably think you were a plant put there to lead them astray. You're a new face, and they'll be suspicious. That's how devious things have become these days in this part of the war. We all start with the premise that nothing is real. Certainly nothing is what it seems to be."

I must have smiled, too.

"You think I'm joking? Well, maybe a little. But when I tell you we have a man picking up Moroccan mule turds for analysis by our weapons boys in London, you'll change your mind—at least about how devious things are. There aren't many good roads in this part of the world, and those few are scattered with mule droppings, so our folks are making small land mines in that shape and color. Big enough to blow up a tire or maybe a tank tread. That's in case the Germans or their buddies decide to come west to attack Morocco."

"English mule turds wouldn't do?"

"Surprisingly not. Different feed results in different color and consistency, you see. Personally, I doubt whether your average German truck driver would know the difference. But our mad scientists are fussy about details."

"What happens if the Germans don't come?"

"Well, then you wouldn't want a job as a road sweeper. And there'll be a few bad days for stray dogs. But the whole point is, not even a humble pile of shit is a humble pile of shit. We and the enemy are thinking creatively, so the idea of planting someone with false information is standard operating procedure. We do it all the time. We have to figure they do too. Now that I think of it, the fact that you're a former private eye may have suggested to Bunny that you were just the right man for this job. Maybe he figured you could tell the phonies from the real guys."

"Well, sir, I have worked the last half-dozen years in Hollywood. I guess if I'm an expert in anything, it's phonies. So I hope Bunny's right."

"Me, too. But if you think the exploding mule turds is a one-off Marx Brothers' idea, there's a scheme in the works to dress up a dead body in an officer's uniform with a set of phony plans and dump him off the shores of Spain, figuring sooner or later he'll drift ashore, the Spanish cops will find him, and the phony plans will eventually get to Adolf. It's not my project, but I've heard about it. So these things do go on. Even so, I would not want you to get arrested."

"Me, either. But I assume we have diplomatic immunity. Doesn't that provide some cover?"

"Up to a point. Which is another way of saying, not exactly. Our diplomatic status with the Spanish—and more importantly, with the Vichy French—has been very useful to our intelligence business. It means that we can send and receive things by diplomatic pouch, which allows for a degree of secrecy in our communication. And we can move around pretty freely through both parts of Morocco and Algeria, for that matter. The president and the State Department took a great deal of flak for recognizing Vichy after the surrender. And you can understand why. But the arrangement has been very helpful to us, so it was another pretty good deal with the Devil— which more or less describes what we do here, daily. On the other hand, we've had a hell of a time setting up a series of secret radio stations, so that we can transmit and receive when the mule shit hits the road. They are technically illegal, even for us attachés. So we have far from a free hand. I suppose you've been briefed on all this political stuff."

"Up to a point."

"Ha! Very good. Speaking of 'up to a point,' are you familiar with Evelyn Waugh? No? Very funny writer. His novel *Scoop* uses that line, which is where I got it. This English press lord, sort of a Beaverbrook character, bosses everyone around and people are afraid to say no to him, so when he asks a tough question they respond with 'Up to a point, Lord Copper,' when the answer is really no."

"I'll look it up. I do read a lot. When there's time."

"You should. Anyway, you have to keep in mind that you are dealing with the Nazis and their stooges—Italian, Spanish, and Vichy French—plus their natives. They don't play by civilized rules. And so, we don't either. They won't necessarily arrest you and put you in jail, but you might end up in a lonely spot in the desert, if they find you doing something they don't like. I don't say this to be melodramatic, once again. But just so that you'll know the situation."

"Yes, sir."

"How do you plan to go about figuring out the river?"

"Aside from going and taking a look, I was hoping for a suggestion or two."

"You're familiar with Samuel Johnson?"

"Yes, but mostly through Bunny."

"Yes, that figures. Well, Johnson said there are two kinds of knowledge—knowledge of the thing itself, and knowledge of where to find out about it. In this case, the second way is the more efficient, seems to me. There's no sense trying to learn every twist and turn and channel, when there's probably someone who already knows it. It'll just be a matter of finding him and persuading him to give you the information."

"That occurred to me as well, sir. There's the added problem that the Sebou is a tidal river, so it will be different at different stages of the tide. It may be navigable only part of the time. Which means local knowledge is a lot more useful than my personal observations."

"Yes. Heraclitus said you can never step into the same river twice. He must have been thinking of a river like the Sebou."

"Yes, sir. He often came to Morocco for the waters."

"Really?"

"Up to a point, Colonel."

"Ah. Good. You can tell a lie with a straight face."

"Thank you, sir."

"Well, when you get to Casablanca, you will contact our man there. Tell him what you're thinking about. He'll know the basics of the assignment and may have some suggestions for you. He's an anthropologist and a Harvard professor. I don't hold that against him. But I warn you, he has a lively imagination. He enjoys this business—maybe more than he should. Likes to run around the desert in native costume. He's the one who dreamed up the exploding mule shit. So I wouldn't accept a cigar from him, if I were you. At least, if you do, don't light it."

"I don't smoke, sir."

"Very wise. We'll fix you up with a car and a driver and all the necessary papers. There's a pretty good road between here and there, which is convenient in one sense and not so good in another, because it makes it easy for the Vichy to watch it and to set up checkpoints wherever they want. There's one at the border between the Spanish and the French sections, of course, but others are ad hoc. Could spring up anywhere once you're in the French zone. But going down you shouldn't have any trouble."

"Thank you, sir."

He looked at me for a moment, obviously making an assessment. He seemed satisfied.

"I hear you did well against the Krauts in the Gulf of Mexico."

"We got a German freighter and the crew of a U-boat."

"Nice work. I just got back from a meeting with the brass who are going to run the Moroccan side of Torch. George Patton's in command. When I came limping into the meeting he said, 'Well, he looks like he's been shot at enough.' To him that was a compliment. I told him I agreed with the 'enough' part, which brought a laugh. I'd never met him before, but he impressed me as someone who knows what he's doing. It's funny how you get these quick impressions. And my quick impression is that you'll do fine in this job."

"I appreciate that, Colonel."

"All you need is a code name. An ideas? Preferences?"

"No, sir. Not offhand."

"I know. You come from Hollywood. How about Beau Geste?"

"Okay by me, sir. Of course, he dies in the end."

"Yes, but he gets the job done. Besides, life doesn't have to imitate art, does it?"

"No, sir. In fact, in my experience, it almost never does."

"Good. Beau Geste it is. How about another drink?"

"That'd be good."

My mouth was a little dry—probably from the desert air.

Chapter Six

THE NEXT MORNING I WAS ON THE ROAD TO CASABLANCA. THE CAR was an old Chevy four-door sedan, but it seemed to be running well. My driver was a civilian hired by the Consulate. His name was Moshe. He appeared to be about fifty, dressed in a very well-worn black suit and tie. His shirt used to be white but had faded badly. He wore a broad-brimmed fedora, shiny with age. He was sallow-skinned and had very dark eyes and a bushy beard that was showing signs of gray.

I was used to standing officer of the deck watches on the bridge of my ship and knew that the enlisted men would not initiate conversation. If you didn't want to talk, the men would be respectfully quiet, and bridge would be silent for your four-hour watch, except for orders to the helm and so on. But if you did feel like talking, and if there was very little going on to worry about, all you had to do was show some interest in anything, and the men would respond. So I understood this arrangement. This driver was not a sailor, but he was an employee of the Consulate, so the same protocol existed.

For the first five or ten minutes or so we rode along in silence, after introductions. I was glad he didn't feel he had to make conversation, like a taxi driver or barber. But it was going to be a long drive, and besides, I was new to the country. Any local information could be useful.

"How did you come to work for the Consulate?" I said. And that turned on the spigot.

"I was a rabbi," he said, "but I have lost my vocation."

"Really? That was careless of you." I smiled to indicate I was not an idiot. It was a favorite joke of mine, stolen from *The Importance of Being Earnest*.

He looked at me skeptically, trying to decide.

"Eh? Oh. You are being humorous," he said finally, grinning. "Ha! Careless. Very good. I will remember that one the next time I see a man with one ear. Yes, I lost my vocation. Now I am a driver for the Americans. Colonel Eddy hired me personally. He thinks that if there is one person you can trust not to be a Nazi, it is a Jew. It is what you call a safe bet."

"I've been told you really can't trust anyone in this country."

"That is also true. It illustrates one of the reasons that I am no longer a rabbi."

"That you can't trust anyone?"

"No, sir. That two things that are opposites can both be true, simultaneously. Or false, mutually."

"That you can't trust anyone and it's safe to trust a Jew?"

"Yes. These sorts of paradoxes used to puzzle and worry me to the point that I simply had to give up thinking about them. I realized I am an atheist who believes in God, and since there was nothing I could do about it, I decided not to think about it anymore."

"I suppose the troubles your people are having in Europe didn't help your faith very much."

"No, it was not that so much. Those things are an old story. We have always believed that the atrocities and persecutions were signs that we are God's chosen people. No, what changed me was a little dog I used to have. His name was Boris. He loved me more than anyone in my family did, but that is understandable. My marriage was arranged, according to our traditions, so there is no shame in the fact that my wife disliked me. I didn't care much for her either. As for the children that came from it, well, they were a mixed blessing, also as usual. But Boris! His devotion was pure and unwavering."

"What kind of dog was he?"

"What kind? Who knows? A mongrel of exceptional breeding. He was my constant companion and very devoted. He had only one eye and so was careful about turning left. But in all other respects, he was a fine dog. One day I was reading a story by one of your people, Jack London. Do you know of him?"

"Yes."

"Well, in it he said something that made think about a great many things. The gist of what he said was that dogs are the only creatures in the world that can actually see their god. Humans. Us. Me. Think of it! I was Boris's deity! And I realized that this was a great responsibility, and I began to take it very seriously. Then Boris got sick and died, and at the end he would look at me with his one sad eye and whimper, as though asking me why I did not lift this terrible burden from him. And of course I could not. So that is when I realized how things really were. It is not that God does not care for us, but that He can't do anything about it."

"God is not omnipotent?"

"Well, sir, there are only two possible answers to that question. The first is—no. He is not. Terrible things happen in the world, but He is not responsible. But on the other hand, if you say that He is omnipotent and yet chooses to do nothing about what goes on, you are on the path to despair and madness. Since there is no way of knowing which is true, I prefer to choose the first and retain my sanity. After all, He is called the father. I am a father, too. When the children were sick, what could I do? And when one of them ran off and married a Gentile, what could I do? When finally they all grew up and went away, what was I supposed to do about it? And when the Russian Gentiles came to the village to burn us out, I could do nothing about what they did.

"It was then that I decided to leave Russia and stop pretending to be a rabbi, so I ended up in this country where they tolerate my kind, if only a little. But this is only a way station on the road to America, God willing. Not that I think God is following my progress with any interest."

"You should do well there. Your English is remarkably good."

Moshe had a thick Russian accent, of course, but that was to be expected.

"Yes. Thank you. I am gifted. I learn languages easily. Besides, as a rabbi I had time to think and write and study. My people thought I was studying the sacred texts, so that I could explain inexplicable things to them, but in fact I was learning English by reading novels and newspapers, because by that time I knew there were no answers in the texts, or if there were, I could not understand them. So I decided it would be a better use of time to learn English, so that I could leave Russia and go to America and make some kind of living."

"I'm surprised you were able to get English books and papers in Russia."

"It wasn't easy, but I had a friend who worked in the city library, until he disappeared, one way or the other. I heard that a policeman took a fancy to his wife, and very soon thereafter my friend was no longer there, or anywhere else, for that matter. For our people, having the matchmaker arrange a beautiful wife for you can be a mixed blessing. Poor Mordechai. I left owing a large library fine for overdue books. In my catalog of guilt feelings, that is one of the smaller ones. If I ever become rich, I will send them a check. If not, well, I will have to live with it."

"Why did you come to Morocco?"

"Ah. Why? I can see you know very little about my people's history."

"I'm a Presbyterian originally from Ohio and recently exiled from Hollywood, California. The only Jews I know are movie producers, and they don't talk to me about Old Testament history.

When they talked to me at all, it was usually about finding a missing girlfriend or taking care of a blackmailer."

"Ah! You were a policeman!"

"A private one. Now and then I'd go to a Jewish funeral, but that was only to be polite to someone I used to know. And all I knew about it was you're supposed to wear a hat."

"That is true. I believe this constant wearing of hats is the reason so many of our people are bald. It is bad for the hair, this lack of air and sunlight." He raised his fedora to show his own shiny dome. "But if God wants you to be bald, what choice is there? Not that I believe He really cares."

"In many of the Christian religions, it is the women who cover their heads in church."

"Yes. That proves my point. That appears to be another of those opposite things that are both true at the same time. If it were really important to God, I am sure He would clear up the confusion. But I am glad to know that the Jews have a community there in Hollywood."

"Yes, you have a community there."

"I had been thinking of Brooklyn, New York, but now I think I would prefer Hollywood, California. You have changed my mind. But you asked why I came to Morocco. The answer is I believed I would be less unwelcome here than other places. It is simple as that."

"And have you been?"

"Up to a point."

Moshe had obviously been spending time with Colonel Eddy, and I said something about that.

"Colonel Eddy? Yes. I do errands for him now and then. 'Up to a point.' It is one of his favorite sayings. He is a very good man. He has promised to help me get to America, somehow."

"Morocco is not quite as congenial as you would like?"

"Well, you see, the local Jews here are Sephardic, which means they originally came from Spain. The refugees from Europe who are fleeing the Nazis, like me, are Ashkenazi. We come from central Europe, Russia and Poland, mostly. The two of us don't necessarily love one another as we should, but we like each other better than anyone else likes either of us. But there are differences. We speak different languages, although Hebrew is of course a common denominator. But in so many ways we are different. Ask a Sephardic for a knish, and you get a blank stare. Ask an Ashkenazi for money, and you get a blank check. Unsigned. Ha! That's a joke. So staying in Morocco does not appeal very much. And there is always the possibility that the Germans will come here, in which case it will be better to be gone. Besides, America is the land of opportunity, so it will be better there, regardless of what happens here."

"Where is your family now? Are they here, too?"

"Ah. Well, the children grew up and moved away somewhere. That was years ago. Life in a Russian *shtetl* has nothing much to offer. Poverty and hard work, seasoned by an occasional pogrom. I don't blame them for leaving, but I have lost touch with them. They never write. They were very ungrateful, although in truth I cannot blame them for that either, because there was little or nothing to be grateful for. My wife, poor woman, was killed in a pogrom two years ago. This was just before the Germans were getting ready to invade Russia. The Russians wanted to get to us before the Nazis arrived and robbed them of the chance. I was hiding in the barn when it happened. I got out at the last minute, just before it collapsed and burned to the ground. I ran into the woods."

"Is it possible your wife survived?"

"No. I saw what happened."

"I'm sorry."

"Yes. It was a very great shame. The world lost a genius at argument. She should have been the rabbi in the family, although such a

thing is not heard of, of course. Her pet name for me was *schnorrer*.
Do you know this word? If you do, I will be surprised."

"No."

"Good. I have come to the point in life when I do not like sur-
prises. So I will explain. A *schnorrer* is a beggar. But not the pathetic
kind of beggar you see on the streets of Tangier. No. The *schnorrer* is
clever and he has a sense of humor, which for a Jew is two eyes in
the same head. Is this a common expression?"

"I've never heard it. Maybe you mean two sides of the same coin."

"That, too. The *schnorrer* is a beggar, because he likes it better
than working. There is an old joke. A *schnorrer* is making his usual
rounds of the rich men in the city, and he goes to the home of one
who has been a reluctant but reliable giver in the past. But when the
schnorrer asks for alms, the rich man says, 'I have had a bad year and
I can only give you half of what I have given you in the past,' and
the *schnorrer* says, '*You're* the one who had the bad year—why should
I suffer?' You see?"

"Yes. It's pretty clear." At least, it was clear on the surface.

"My wife knew something about me when she called me that. I
had to smile, even though she did not mean it as a compliment, particularly. In thirty years of marriage the only compliments we ever
shared were when we boiled a chicken, which was something rare
and only happened when the bird grew too old and stopped laying
eggs. But in that rare event I would say something like 'This is good
chicken soup.' And in return she would sometimes say to me, 'You
don't smell as bad as usual.' This does not remind anyone of the Song
of Solomon."

"No. Nor the lines of a romantic poet. But now I think you're
going to tell me that, in spite of everything, you grew to love her in
your own way."

"Me? No. Not at all. She was very disagreeable. And her gruff
behavior toward me was not an act; she really did dislike me. Of

course, I was shocked and saddened to see her die, but I must say, when I thought about it afterwards, I realized it certainly simplified things. Especially because the Russians also burned down our house. And stole the cow. There was no reason to stay, and many reasons to go."

"So how in hell did you get out and find your way here?"

He smiled and touched his nose and raised his eyebrows, meaningfully.

"Well, Lieutenant, my wife was right, you see. She married a *schnorrer*."

Chapter Seven

THE ROAD TO CASABLANCA REMINDED ME OF CALIFORNIA 101 that runs north and south between the high desert on one side and the blue Pacific on the other. Except this was the moody Atlantic. Still, the sun was shining brilliantly, there were no clouds in the sky, and the landscape was familiar-looking, greens and light browns, scrub trees and the bush the French called *maquis*, and in the distance to the east, the peaks of the Atlas Mountains. There was still some snow on the highest peaks, and I supposed it must be there year-round.

All in all, the country had become beautiful, and I began to lose the feeling of being a stranger in a strange land. It didn't look anything like the desert scenes in *Beau Geste*, thankfully.

I couldn't help noticing that the surf was very strong in places—sometimes ten to fifteen feet—and I wondered how a landing craft would be able to get safely through it, unload its troops, and then retract and go back to a transport ship for another load. Simply getting turned around would be risky in these rollers. The navy coxswains handling the boats would have to be very good at their jobs. Maybe the brass would find beaches where it wasn't so rough. And we were still a couple of hundred miles from Casablanca. Maybe it would be better there. But this was the Atlantic, and it was far more unpredictable than the Pacific.

There weren't many vehicles on the road, but here and there we would pass a mule-driven wagon loaded with wares and driven by a dark man in a striped robe and a kind of turban.

"Berber," said Moshe. "A merchant headed for market. Perhaps to buy, perhaps to sell—and certainly to cheat, if possible."

"You don't think much of the Arab locals."

"I think of them exactly what they think of me. We have a mutual admiration society. It is in the blood of all Semites to bargain and look for an edge. And to be nimble when someone is not looking. It is expected. There is no fault attached."

"All Semites? I thought only Jews were Semites."

"Many people think that. But, no. Arabs are Semites, too. We are very close relatives. That is one reason why we don't get along."

"So when someone who hates Jews claims to be an anti-Semite, he is being narrow-minded and limiting himself."

"Well, let us just say he is missing a lot of opportunities. You watch. When Hitler and the Nazis finish with one tribe, they will move on to the next. When it comes to hatred, they know what they're doing."

"Then why are some Arabs giving Hitler a hand in the Middle East? They are, you know."

"Yes. And why? If you are sitting on an anvil, make friends with the hammer."

"That sounds vaguely biblical."

"It is from the Book of Moshe."

"I thought you were going to say the enemy of my enemy is my friend."

"That, too. But it is not as colorful."

We came to the border checkpoint and passed through the Spanish side with no trouble. Our papers were entirely legitimate, after all, and issued by the American Consulate. The guards on the French side were a little less polite, I suppose because we were coming into their country, instead of leaving it.

I noticed that Moshe seemed nervous. The border guards were native troops and looked at him with suspicion and distaste. He was sweating pretty freely as we presented our papers. He did not look the guards in the eye, but I was pretty casual and polite with them, which is easy to do, when your papers are good. Otherwise, it's not so easy. I imagined Moshe had plenty of memories of crossing hostile borders with only the flimsiest of documents. But we got through after only a cursory search of our vehicle.

"I don't like policemen," said Moshe, as we accelerated away from the checkpoint. "They have always been birds of ill omen. And often they have been the omen come true."

"Maybe you should wear a fez and native clothes."

"Maybe, but that would be going against our tradition."

"I thought you said God didn't care."

"Yes. I believe that. But what if I'm wrong?"

"Good point. And if more people in the world asked themselves that question now and then, we'd all be better off."

"You are a philosopher, Lieutenant."

"Not really. I'm a Presbyterian from Hollywood by way of Ohio."

He smiled and was quiet for a few minutes. He was thinking about something.

"I believe the Presbyterians are Calvinists," he said, finally.

"That's the rumor."

"And they, meaning you, are therefore members of the Elect?"

"So they say."

"It must be very comforting."

"That's why I seem so relaxed."

"Maybe when I get to America, I will convert. It would certainly remove a lot of worrying."

"Maybe. But what if your people were right all along, and all those rituals you observe were correct and mandatory? What then? You'd be like the professional athlete who left his team in disgust just before they went on to win the championship."

"Even so, I wonder if they'd have me."

"Who, the Presbyterians? Why not?"

He looked at me and smiled knowingly.

"You know why not, Lieutenant. If you cut down a tree and saw it into timber and build a house with it and paint the house white, the house is still made of wood, the very same that made the tree. And if there comes a great flood and the house is washed away, as it floats downstream, it is still wood. Or if a great storm comes along and blows the house to pieces, the pieces are scattered, but they are still wood. It is only when it is burned to ashes or eaten by termites that it ceases to be what it was and becomes something else."

"And what is that?"

He shrugged.

"I don't know. Nothing. A memory."

"Thank you for adding a touch of gloom to an otherwise lovely day, Moshe."

"I apologize, Lieutenant. It is my penance for the library books, I suppose. Perhaps when I send a check for the fines, I will become lighthearted."

The road ran along the Atlantic shoreline for the first half of the trip but then swerved inland about six miles and followed the course of a river that was flowing almost due south. This was the Sebou, according to my map. The map showed the river making two hairpin turns. From its source in the northeast the Sebou ran south but then turned 180 degrees to flow north for a few miles. There it turned south again and ran to the sea.

At the base of the first hairpin was the city of Port Lyautey, named after the French general who more or less conquered and developed Morocco into a semi-European colony. There was a highway bridge across the river where it started its bend. The airfield sat alongside the left bank of the river as it headed back north. There were several French air force planes parked on the concrete runways and near the hangars. The city itself was modern, built only recently by the French, and it was protected by trench works and artillery and machine-gun emplacements. There were long buildings that were obvious barracks, and there were men drilling on the parade grounds in front.

Our intelligence reports said that there was at least a regiment of French troops there—natives and Foreign Legion. There was no particular attempt to disguise any of this. I had the feeling the defenses and military buildings were there primarily to forestall or counteract domestic rebellions.

Morocco had a history of Berber unrest and revolt. The Rif War in the 1920s had lasted a long seven years, with casualties on both sides running into the tens of thousands. It was a grim business, so the colonial governments of both Spain and France were well advised to take Berber hostility seriously. It didn't seem to me that this French installation was anticipating any modern European enemy, and that therefore concealment and camouflage were not thought to be necessary. In fact, maybe they thought the more powerful the facilities were to the naked eye, the more intimidating and discouraging they would be to potential native rebels. The town and airfield were also protected by a marshy lagoon between the city and the coastline, which was six miles away as the crow flies.

As I looked at the formidable installations in Port Lyautey, I wondered—just as all the senior military planners were wondering—if, when we landed here in force, the French would fight. Or would they greet us with kisses on both cheeks and bottles of champagne? They were supposed to be our allies; weren't they? Then I remembered Mers-el-Kébir.

From Port Lyautey the river wound twelve miles to the outlet in the Atlantic. And near the outlet of the river, on the north bank, there was a hillside fort called the Kasbah. Despite the scent of romance around the word, it really just meant "fort." There was another one in Casablanca. The Kasbah at the river mouth was an ancient pile built centuries ago by the Portuguese when they were here, trading and running things. The fort was there to protect the river entrance and the little trading village of Mehdia on the opposite bank.

I couldn't see the fort from where we were, but it was marked on the map. I thought ruefully of my code name. Was the Foreign Legion guarding that fort? Was there an evil Russian sergeant there terrorizing the Legionnaires? I remembered that scene in the movie when he shouts to the men, "Keep shooting, you scum! You'll get a chance yet to die with your boots on!" Did the Legionnaires all wear those hats with sun flaps? I was only mildly curious and would not be unhappy if I never found out. And then I remembered listening to a record of Edith Piaf singing a song called "Mon Légionnaire." I wondered how she was dealing with the occupation of Paris.

I could tell nothing by looking at the river. That was too bad. Life would have been far easier if along some stretch of the river there were rapids that indicated rocks or even riffled water that showed shoaling. But as far as I could see in both directions, the water was smooth and dark, from bank to bank. A flyover photo couldn't reveal anything of value; the water was too black—maybe from an excess of silt, maybe from discharges upstream. Maybe from minerals. Who knows? All I knew was that it was black.

On the other hand, the city was called *Port* Lyautey, which indicated that it was capable of receiving shipping. But how large? What was the maximum draft? The French had built it in this spot. Why? Was it because of the terrain and its natural defenses, or was it because it had sufficient depth to receive deepwater vessels? Or both?

But maybe it really wasn't a "port" after all, not in the sense of being an active commercial hub. From what little I knew about Morocco from my hasty reading, a large commercial port in this spot seemed hardly necessary, since only sixty miles or so south lay

Casablanca, which had been built by the French into a modern and very busy port—the same port that sheltered the French navy ships, including the massive battleship *Jean Bart*. Maybe the only function of "Port" Lyautey was the airfield and the military installation. The town and base there could be supplied by river barges and by the roads and the railroad that ran strategically from Marrakesh through Casablanca to Port Lyautey and then headed east toward Fez and Algeria. Commercially, there didn't seem to be any reason for Port Lyautey to exist. Militarily, however, it made some sense.

Given the heavy military presence and the fact that the river itself gave absolutely no clues about its depth, I was a little discouraged. The only shipping I could see was in the form of lighters and barges, most of which could have floated on a wet lawn. Worse, as far as I could see, there were no channel buoys. If it were possible to navigate this river, anyone bringing foreign ships of any size from the ocean twelve miles upstream to this port would have to know the river in all its tidal moods, curves, and shifting bottoms. He would have to be a river pilot. All ports servicing foreign shipping have local pilots living and working at the entrance, and they board the visiting ships and guide them into port. There was not a modern port worthy of the name in all the world that did not have such men available. It was in the interest of all parties not to have shipping running aground and clogging or tearing up the channels. In almost all ports the visiting vessel had no choice in the matter; it was the local law that you must use the local pilot.

But those rules did not apply during war.

"I see that you are very interested in the situation around Port Lyautey, Lieutenant."

"Well, I'm a tourist at heart."

"Of course."

I hadn't been briefed on the overall plan of the North African invasion. My orders were simple—find out about the river. But it was clear that this spot, which was maybe sixty miles north of Casablanca, would be one invasion point. It was also clear that the primary objective of the whole campaign was the city of Casablanca itself, not just because the French navy was there, but also because it was a modern Atlantic port that would be vital for landing supplies and reinforcements. Those supplies were important not just for this operation but on an ongoing basis as we pushed east, evicted Rommel, and made plans to cross the Med for Europe.

So if the planners wanted Port Lyautey, it could only be part of a larger plan to capture Casablanca. There would be a coordinated attack on both locations, and perhaps others, too. We would not want these French troops or French air force planes coming south to oppose an amphibious landing that would be tricky enough going against Casablanca's existing defenses. Port Lyautey would have to be neutralized, one way or the other.

That gave me a slightly uncomfortable feeling. I had diplomatic immunity of a kind, but if I should get arrested, snooping around the Sebou, even the dullest Gestapo agent could put two and two together and draw the same conclusions I did. They wouldn't even have to get out the pliers or hot tongs. My simply being there would probably tell the tale.

In less than two hours we arrived in Casablanca. You could see why it was called that, although from a distance some of the buildings were a little off-white from age and weather. Still, the modern buildings were shining in the afternoon sun, and the overall impression was of a white city shimmering in the heat beside the blue Atlantic. I wondered if the producers shooting the movie would bother getting any location shots. It would look good, but I knew they wouldn't bother. Hollywood could build a replica cheaper than sending a camera crew to North Africa.

French general Hubert Lyautey was responsible for turning Casablanca into a modern European-style city—at least in the sections that surrounded the old Arab town and the Jewish quarter. He was the first provincial governor, and he knew what he wanted and how to do it. So over the years of the early part of the century he had built wide boulevards and graceful government buildings, hotels, and businesses that looked more like Nice's white-wedding-cake architecture than Arab North Africa. Rather than let the natives spoil the scene, he built walls around the Arab quarter, which was called the medina, and around the adjacent Jewish quarter, called the mellah. These were not ghettos in the Hitlerian sense; people were not sealed in them. But the walls did indicate to the locals where their place was and where their homes were to stay. These sectors retained their Old World narrow streets and winding alleys, their dark corners where intrigue was expected, their cafés and open-air shops that made much of the medina seem like a shadowy, congested bazaar. Arabs and Jews could come and go freely throughout the entire city; Lyautey just didn't want their teeming, unhealthy masses to ooze permanently into his lovely new design. Local color was fine, but only up to a point. He also built the port into a modern commercial center and constructed extensive breakwaters and a jetty that protected the port from the whims of the Atlantic. The good marshal did all of this in about a dozen years, from 1912 to 1925. And Casablanca's population of Europeans, mainly French, of course, grew from almost none to half of the city's total of 350,000.

We drove around the medina and the mellah into the new European suburb of Anfa.

"Colonel Eddy wanted me to take you first to Mr. King's villa," said Moshe. "From there I assume I will take you to the Anfa Hotel, which is new and very fine. There, if you look to the right, you will see it. It looks like a ship that has wandered onto a boulevard."

I knew this was the plan, and I knew David King was expecting me. His code name was Markoff.

Chapter Eight

"Beau Geste, I presume." King was smiling as he met me in the hallway of his villa. We shook hands.

"It's only temporary."

"Most things are. Colonel Eddy briefed me by radio on your meeting, so I'm at least that much up-to-date. Pleasant trip?"

"Better than expected."

"Yes, it's an interesting country. Very beautiful in spots. Wait here a minute. I'll tell Moshe to find something to do with himself and come back when you need a ride to the hotel."

"How will he know?"

"I don't know. But he will. Actually, he'll probably park the car across the street and spend the time thinking over his sins. Or wishing he had more sins to think about."

When he came back we settled into the comfortable chairs of his living room, which seemed to house a collection of very fine things that did not fit together. As I soon began to understand, this was by design, and perfectly in tune with King's tastes and attitudes. He agreed to take the job only after the State Department had agreed to ship his furniture, books, and artwork here. And he had rented this suburban villa not only for security reasons, but also because it was in the middle of the fashionable nightlife of the city. If that seemed to be a contradiction, he didn't seem to care. He enjoyed the comforts and convenience.

There were the inevitable ornate tiles on the floor and tapestries on the wall and the Moorish arches leading to other rooms, but the furniture seemed like something out of a very rich college fraternity house—well-used leather couches and chairs and bookshelves, and on the walls, photographs of men in uniform or arranged in rows in front of a college building. Absurdly, there was a Harvard pennant tacked to the wall. The bookshelves were crammed with good volumes next to paperbacks—African history and mystery novels, hunting stories and rhapsodies about fly fishing. And there were a few mementos—a Webley .45 caliber revolver, a short scimitar, a boar's tusk, a piece of marble from some ancient site or other. And on one of the white walls there was also a stunning photo of a nude woman's torso, shot from mid-thigh to the neck.

"That's an Alfred Stieglitz portrait of Georgia O'Keeffe," said King. "You wouldn't know it was Georgia, because he doesn't show her head. But it is perhaps the most perfect woman's body I've ever seen. I saw the picture in New York and had to have a copy. I hope to meet her one day. Stieglitz is old and she might be ready for a bit of variety. Have you ever seen a better body? I haven't."

"No. I agree with you."

"I've never met her, but I've seen other pictures of her. She's not conventionally pretty, but I believe you could get used to that. In fact, with a little imagination you could believe she was beautiful. After all, that's one of the things the imagination is good for."

There was also an eight-by-ten photo of King himself on one of the tables. He was wearing a fez and a loose, native-looking shirt with one of those curved Arab daggers stuck in a sash. He had an impressive mustache with pointed tips that made him look like some storybook Turkish pasha or something.

He noticed that I was looking at it.

"Quite the lad, there, eh? I keep it to remind me."

"Of what?"

"Oh, things. You know—the days before we had to go around playing diplomat in white linen suits and stiff collars. Has to be done, of course, but you wish for the old days now and then."

"Colonel Eddy mentioned that you were in the Foreign Legion."

"Yes. Very exotic. I joined up in 1914 when it was clear we weren't interested in getting into the war. When we finally did, I moved over to our army. Usually you have to sign up for five years with the Legion, but they were kind enough to let me shift over to our gang. A gesture to Franco-American solidarity, I suppose."

Eddy had given me some background on King, who was another of those half-mad American adventurers who were every bit the equal of their British counterparts. He left Harvard to join the Foreign Legion and was sent to the trenches in France, where he was wounded twice and blown up by an artillery shell, buried alive in the collapsed trench. They dug him out at the last possible minute. He had a bad eye with a drooping lid that gave him a satirical expression which fit nicely with his sardonic attitude toward life in general, and the war in particular, although his contempt and hatred for the Germans was sincere enough. Well, that was understandable. They'd tried to kill him three different times. He was about fifty and seemed perfectly at ease, as if he had found the perfect job for his taste and time of life.

"You've lost the mustache," I said.

"Didn't lose it. That would have been careless. Do you know the line 'To lose one parent is a tragedy. To lose both looks like—'"

"Carelessness."

"Bravo. One of my favorites."

"Mine, too. Is it safe to talk here? They said in Tangier that almost everything was bugged."

"It's all right here. The domestic staff are all navy guys. And we're very sure there aren't any microphones around. What's on your mind?"

"We passed right through Port Lyautey," I said. "It looks like it might be a challenge, if it comes to a fight."

"Yes, the old boy knew what he was doing when the place was built. General Lyautey, I mean. In the Legion he's still referred to as

Tinkerbell, in some circles. But it's said with good humor, because by French standards he was a pretty good soldier and administrator, despite being a pansy."

"Really? In the French army?"

"Oh, it was an open secret. When he was sent to Morocco people said it was the right place for him, because the Arabs are pretty casual about that sort of thing. Many of them, anyway. He was famous for having a cluster of handsome young officers on his staff. His wife used to tease them that she'd cuckolded them, on the mornings after she'd serviced the old boy. He had catholic tastes but not Catholic scruples. Ha! A pun. On second thought, maybe he did."

"Well, anyway, I was able to get a few glimpses of the Sebou. But I couldn't tell a thing about how navigable it might be. There were no ships of any size in port and no channel markings."

"I'm not surprised. It might take a few nighttime excursions and a little poking around to figure what the odds are of using it. We'll get you fitted out in a burnoose and turban, and provide you with a camel and a native guide named Ahmed, and some hashish and money for bribes. Nothing to it. Actually, I have some more practical ideas about it. But let's save the shop talk. What do you say we go out? You might like a bit of local color, and besides, my steward cannot for the life of him make a decent martini. He's from Oklahoma, where they don't know about such things."

"Sounds good." The way he talked about burnooses and camels made me think he was joking. I hoped so.

"I generally go out around this hour," he said. "The Gestapo boys follow me everywhere, and they expect it. Being Krauts, they get nervous when things don't go according to schedule. That's why they'll lose the war. Or win it. We'll have to wait and see about that. There's a good nightclub only a couple of blocks from here. It's called Charlie's Blue Water Café. Everybody who's anybody goes there."

"Really?"

"Well, maybe not everyone. No film stars or royalty, and not many millionaires. But all the best spies and their lackeys go there, along with some well-heeled refugees trying to buy their passage out of here or win enough at roulette to bribe the necessary officials for documents—all of which creates a certain atmosphere of intrigue and excitement. They should make a movie about it."

"They are."

"Really? Wonderful! And the women are worth seeing. That's the real reason to go. Quite a stunning chanteuse, especially. Not much of a singer, but that's not important. Eddy tells me you used to be a Hollywood private eye."

"That's true."

"Do you have a gun?"

"Yes. A thirty-eight."

"I thought I noticed the bulge in your cuff."

"I picked up the habit from the cops in LA. An ankle holster's more comfortable than carrying one in a belt or shoulder."

"It's good to have one. You never know in this town. Well, let's go, shall we? You'll like this place."

We walked a couple of blocks. As soon as we left his front door two men in black fedoras and black leather trench coats started following us. King turned and grinned and waved at them.

"We're off to Charlie's, Fritz," he yelled to them.

"They certainly aren't trying to hide," I said. "Those trench coats seem like something out of a B movie, speaking of movies."

"Yes. You and I know that, but they think it makes them look sinister, instead of just ridiculous. They must sweat like pigs in this weather. But you know, the Gestapo really are just a collection of thugs without any imagination. Most of them were walking the beat and passing out parking tickets before the war. They would be heartbroken if Himmler took away their leather coats. Morale would plummet. It doesn't matter to us. We assume we're always being followed, so they could dress up as ballerinas and it wouldn't make a bit of difference."

King had said I'd like this saloon. And I did.

The painted sign above the Moorish archway announced Charlie's Blue Water Café. The doorman in the uniform of a Hungarian hussar greeted us with a salute, and we were ushered into the inner sanctum. The room was about as large as a public ballroom but partially broken up into alcoves and booths. The decor was a mixture of Arabian nights and a cheap Monte Carlo casino, with potted palms, more archways, and a high ceiling made of smoke-darkened exposed beams. There were craps and roulette tables, and in the rear, a few card tables with serious-looking fat men studying their cards and smoking cigars.

The lighting was dim, and the room was crowded with fashionable people and some local natives selling things out of trays—flowers for the ladies, tobacco, Moorish souvenirs. The noise was just a little short of deafening. The croupier was yelling *Faites vos jeux!* as he spun the wheel, and the dance band was playing "Begin the Beguine." People were laughing or groaning when red turned up instead of black, and there were people at small tables in the corners and shadows with their heads together, plotting something, either romance or escape or payment of some amount for something illegal. And over the room was a haze of cigarette smoke that mingled with the heavy scent of perfume and, worse, men's cologne. Waiters in tuxedos that were shiny at the elbows wandered through the crowd carrying trays of drinks or ice buckets for champagne. On the right of the main entrance was a long bar that was crowded with well-dressed men and stylish women standing or sitting and drinking cocktails.

"Josephine Baker sang here once or twice," said King, as we waited for the maître d' to come over and guide us to a table. "Poor woman. She caught a frightful bug of some kind and has been in the hospital here for months. People say she's lost a lot of weight, which is a shame on several levels. She was actually useful to our side for a while after the Vichy deal. Smuggled a few documents between here and Lisbon in her underwear."

"Really?"

"Oh, yes. She wasn't having any of the Vichy line. She was more Parisian than Parisians. Not like her old partner, Chevalier. He'd tap-dance naked for Hitler himself, if you promised him a good hotel room and room service."

The maître d', a smiling fat man who went by the name of Cuddles, came up to us and enthused, his jowls and wattles shimmying.

"Mr. King. It is good to see you. It has been a while." Cuddles had a thick accent of some kind, something I couldn't place.

"Yes, almost twenty-four hours. How about something fairly close to the band. I've told my friend about your chanteuse."

"Yes, of course. Right this way." He guided us to a small table to the right of the bandstand.

"Is Charlie in tonight?" asked King. Did I detect a note of sarcasm? It was hard to tell with King.

"Not tonight, sir," said Cuddles. "He has gone off somewhere with one of the chorus girls from the Norwegian Parrot. Beautiful girl. I think he is besotted. Is that the correct word?"

"It is, if that's what you mean to say. Too bad, though."

When Cuddles had gone off, King said, "There really is no Charlie. He's a fictional character. Cuddles is the actual owner, and he likes to promote Charlie as a shadowy figure of romance. It gives the place glamour and tone, he thinks. It only works with transients, but then, almost everyone in here is a transient. All the rest are spies or cops or government people. They all know the true story but don't care."

"What's his accent?"

"God knows. Sometimes he claims to be a Lett. Who the hell knows what a Lett sounds like? Most people think 'Lett' only means 'take the first serve over again.' Other times he says he's exiled royalty from Montenegro—and a distant cousin of Njegos. Heard of him?"

"No."

"Some sort of Serbo-Croatian poet or something. Anyway, Cuddles should really consider moving to America, the land of self-invention."

"Yes, Hollywood would be ideal. No one there has the name or history he was born with. And no one cares."

"Even you?"

"I'm the exception."

Just then the music stopped, the house lights dimmed, and the bandleader/emcee stepped to the microphone. A spotlight shone on him.

"Mesdames and messieurs, it is time for the featured part of our program. Please welcome the star attraction of Charlie's Blue Water Café, Mademoiselle Yvonne Dubonnet!"

The audience applauded and there were a few whistles and knuckles wrapping on tables which indicated Germans giving approval. Into the spotlight stepped a tall woman in a shimmering silver dress. Her hair was cut short and was the color of her dress. She wore vivid red lipstick and dark glasses. She looked in the direction of our table and seemed to recognize King, who nodded and smiled sardonically at her.

The band struck up a familiar French song, "Mon Légionnaire." Yvonne began to sing. Her voice was more like a throaty spoken monologue, but it didn't matter. She was beautiful in a slightly dissipated or degenerate way, her voice saying unmistakably that she was tired from too many disappointments, too many failed love affairs, too many late-night absinthes and Gauloises cigarettes. As a chanteuse, therefore, she was perfect. And it was by careful design.

I do not know his name,
I do not know anything about him
He loved me all night
my legionnaire
And leaving me to my destiny
He left in the morning

It sounds better in French.

Anyway, she finished the song and the audience raved and Yvonne smiled a sad smile of a woman grown used to lost love, and she nodded and stepped down from the stage and walked over to our table. King and I both stood up.

"Good evening, Monsieur King," she said, pronouncing all three syllables of "evening."

"Good evening, Yvonne," King said. "Lovely song. Were you singing it for me, your legionnaire?"

"Who else?" She smiled at King, beautifully insincere, and kissed him on his cheeks, *à la mode française.*

"And may I present a friend of mine, Lieutenant Fitzhugh," said King.

She turned to me and smiled again, thoroughly composed.

"Hello, Riley."

"Hello, Amanda."

Chapter Nine

"You've changed your hair."

"Yes. Do you like it?"

"I'm not sure. You used to remind me of butterscotch. Now you seem more like an ice princess."

"Only with my clothes and makeup on. The real me is the way you remember, I hope."

"Yes. Exactly."

There was no doubt about that.

We were in my room at the Anfa Hotel, stretched out on the oversized bed, naked and satisfied, for the moment.

"I've missed you," she said.

"And who could blame you?"

"Beast. Were you terribly sad when I left last time?"

"Brokenhearted."

"Really?"

"No. As you said, it was just—"

"*One of those things?*" She sang it in her throaty chanteuse way.

"Yes, if you like. After all, you must remember what you said at the time—a harmless bit of shagging. Or was it *friendly* shagging? I forget."

"Either way, darling. Like tonight?"

"Sure."

"Oh, dear. I was rather hoping it was more than that tonight."

"Were you? Well, in that case, yes, it was much more than that."

"Liar. But thank you for saying it. Were you surprised to see me here?"

"Not as much as you'd think. I ran into our friend Bunny in London, and he told me you were here."

"Oh? How did you happen to see him?" she asked.

I could sense her antenna quivering, just a bit. Some quiet alarm bell had gone off. I was not at all surprised. She could have been acting. You never knew with Amanda—which could be a song title.

"Oh, purely by accident," I said. "I was in Hatchards bookshop on Piccadilly, and he wandered in. We went to the Ritz and had a drink for old times' sake, and he mentioned it."

"I see. Quite a coincidence."

"I suppose so. What are you doing here?"

"I might ask you the same thing, darling."

"Me. Nothing much. After you left Los Angeles I joined the navy and war came along and I was assigned to a ship that was bombed on the way to England in a convoy, and they took me off and made me a naval attaché here. Don't ask me why. I have no idea what I'm supposed to be doing. Just got here."

"Oh, I see. Were you hurt? I don't see any scars."

"Just a few scratches. I was luckier than some. Whatever happened to your Prussian friend, Joachim?"

"Embs? Who knows? He's probably somewhere on the Russian front, wishing he'd never heard of Hitler."

"And what happened to your job with the British foreign office?"

"Got the sack. And afterwards, I didn't want to go home and face all those disapproving looks from friends and family. Even in the best of families, it's considered poor form to shoot your husband, especially if he dies. It's one thing to pepper him accidentally on the grouse moors and quite another to plug him with a thirty-eight. It was your thirty-eight, as I remember."

"Yes, it was. I lent it to you to scare away intruders."

"Yes. You were very good to me then, darling. I remember all of it."

"But how did you end up here?"

"A friend invited me to come with him to Casablanca, so I did, unfortunately. That didn't work out. He turned out to be a rat, and I was kind of marooned here. Luckily I got a job at Charlie's. And so, voilà! Yvonne Dubonnet. Apparently Dubonnet's some kind of cheap French wine."

"Why not just be Amanda Billingsgate?"

"An English chanteuse? Have you ever heard of such a thing?"

"Vera Lynn?"

"Really, darling. She's a singer, not a chanteuse."

I didn't believe any of her story, except the part about Vera Lynn, and I don't think she cared whether I did or not. We both knew that neither of us was going to tell the whole truth, so there was no sense wasting creative energy on elaborate lies. As most people know, elaborate lies are a problem, because you always have to remember what you've said. A bare minimum of the truth may or may not be more virtuous, but usually it's more convenient. The best is saying almost nothing at all.

Amanda was good at that, too. I was pretty sure she wasn't lured here by some cad and then abandoned to a tearful fate. And I was very sure she would never have stayed in Casablanca to make her way as a singer. She was a lousy singer, even for an imitation French cabaret chanteuse. Somebody sent her here and got her this job at Charlie's, because it was a good cover for what she was really here for. She was beautiful and could fake it, so the customers didn't care. Charlie's was a good place to pick up information of all sorts and to make contacts. She was a spy, and she knew I knew it. But she was wonderful in bed and had a lithe and muscular body and enjoyed sharing it. And although she was a phony in much of what she said and did, she was not a faker in bed; she was unfailingly honest about that. I think that was because she thought making love, at least, was important, while almost nothing else was. And so her murmured sounds of appreciation made making love to her that much sweeter—that, and the fact that she might well be an enemy agent. That added an element of spice. Whether it was real or imagined didn't really matter.

When I first met her in Los Angeles, she and her husband, the Honorable Freddie Billingsgate, were assigned to the LA office of the British Consulate. One night at their home in Bel Air, she had put a bullet in his forehead. She said that in the dark she'd thought he was a violent intruder, and everybody agreed to agree that it was an accident. I had my doubts, but I helped her with the case, and her government more or less covered everything up and sent her home. The facts were never quite clear.

Nothing about Amanda was ever quite clear. But I was glad to see her again. Except for the platinum hair, she was exactly what I remembered. There was something about the color of her skin and her brown eyes that reminded people of butterscotch. That hadn't changed. Well, it had only been a couple of years. And if I was being honest with myself, I actually had missed her for a while, when she left LA.

"Who was the guy you came here with?"

"Him? Oh, no one you'd know. You know how that is. Why? Are you jealous?"

"Like Othello."

"I suppose I should know who that is, darling, but I told you when we first met that upper-class English girls don't know anything except 'what's done' and 'what's not done.'"

"He was a character in a play by one of your people. He killed his wife in a fit of jealousy. It was pretty much a mistake, and he was sorry afterwards."

"Oh, yes. I remember now. Something about a pillow. Well, then, I suppose he and I have something in common, don't we. Well, if I've learned anything, it's that people don't feel sorry for you, when you become a widow the way I did."

"People can be so cruel."

"I know. But as we say in Paree, *c'est la vie*. I'm hungry," she said, sitting up in bed. "Let's have room service. Want to? We'll eat starkers the way we used to—once the waiter is gone." She always liked to have room service and eat it in the nude. I didn't mind, either. "I wonder if they have cold lobster. I know they have champagne. This is France after all, almost."

"I'd settle for scrambled eggs."

"Mmm, yes. That sounds good. Champagne and scrambled eggs, fruit, toast, jam and fresh butter. Maybe there'll be some butter left over. Remember?"

It was three a.m. before we finally fell asleep.

In the morning I was reminded of that old blues song—"I woke up and found you gone." It was nine a.m. and the other side of the bed was empty and not even still warm. Her pillow smelled good, but that was the only trace of Amanda.

As I got dressed I wondered where she was and what she was doing right now. With Amanda there was no use speculating. She could be at Charlie's rehearsing with the band or on a plane heading for somewhere in Europe. Time would tell, maybe. Probably.

As I was dressing, I also thought about Martha and wondered what *she* was doing, if she had made it back to Havana yet or was still sitting on someone's lap at *Collier's*, sweet-talking him out of another assignment. And I wondered if I should be feeling guilty about last night. But that was only a fleeting and feckless question. There were a few things that I never wanted to be, and feckless was one of them. Besides, Martha and I had made no promises other than to try not to get killed, and to write. Maybe I'd write her a letter later today.

The truth was, I didn't feel at all guilty about last night. I didn't even feel guilty about not feeling guilty. It was something for the memory bank, something to draw from on cold, rainy nights in the future, something not to tell the grandchildren about. Amanda had a way of whispering—"Yes . . . just there"—that was something you would not forget, and didn't want to.

I had agreed to meet King at his villa at ten that morning. And when I went downstairs and out the front door of the hotel, there was Moshe, waiting.

"Good morning, Lieutenant," he said.

"Good morning, Moshe. Pleasant evening?"

"Among my people, yes. In the district they call the mellah."

"You have friends there?"

"Up to a point. But the cafés there are congenial, and I have found it convenient to rent a small room there. Colonel Eddy has me come to Casablanca quite often. Between Mr. King and the Colonel, I go back and forth quite often."

"That's funny. I thought you seemed uncomfortable at the border."

"I was. Policemen make me nervous. It is cowardly, I know, but I cannot help it. Still, it is a good job, so I put up with my fears and my self-contempt."

"Heard any good jokes lately?"

"Yes." He looked over at me and smiled.

Point to Moshe. As a former private eye, I should be ashamed for asking a poorly worded question.

It was only a short drive to King's villa.

"I will be available when you are finished," said Moshe.

I didn't bother asking how he would know.

"Have you had enough coffee?" King said, when we were seated in his comfortable living room.

"Yes, thanks."

"You're aware that our girl Yvonne is someone to be careful with."

"I've known that for a couple of years. If she asked the time of day, she'd have an ulterior motive."

"Good. Just so you know. I sometimes feed her tidbits of phony information. She probably passes it along to whoever's paying her at the moment. What do you think of her singing?"

"Terrible. But she looks good doing it."

"Yes, and more often than not, that's all that's required in this life. I suppose coming from Hollywood you would know that better than I. Well, let's get down to business. I understand that you only got to North Africa a couple of days ago. So I'm not sure how much you know about what we're doing and how we go about it."

"Not much."

"Okay. Let's start at the beginning. The clowns in the leather raincoats are managed by the German Armistice Commission. They're middle-level Nazis who've been sent here ostensibly to make sure the French are living up to the terms of the surrender agreement. There's one of these groups in all the French colonies. Even though America's at war with Germany now, we're here because, before we got into it, Roosevelt had the foresight to recognize Vichy. A lot of people didn't like that—including that ass, de Gaulle—and said he was collaborating with the Nazis, which was pretty much true. But he figured we'd have a better chance of keeping Vichy neutral, if we maintained contact. Which we have. So we are diplomats in a neutral country, and the Krauts are here, too, watching us and everyone else. And even though the United States is now at war with Germany, we diplomats coexist on the surface and do everything possible beneath the surface to bugger the other's fiendish plans and devices."

"Strange."

"That is the word for this situation. Our head diplomat in North Africa is a guy called Robert Murphy, and before we got into the war, he made a deal with the Vichy government to send humanitarian food and medical supplies to North Africa—at Vichy's request— on the condition that none of it would be sent on to any of the belligerent parties. And to make sure everything was on the up and up, the State Department appointed twelve vice consuls whose job it was to monitor these shipments and make sure they got to starving French colonies and nowhere else. At that point these twelve, known modestly as the Twelve Apostles, were recruited by the OSS to do a little work on the side, since we could travel freely and had access to the ports, and the railways and roadways. We could go pretty much where we liked in the role of inspectors."

"You are one of the twelve."

"At your service. You can imagine that this situation is a little tricky, diplomatically. You have the Vichy French, the Germans, and the Allies all here—although the Brits are not especially welcome. The big worry right now is that the Germans will finally decide to take over all of France, instead of just the top half—as well as Algeria and Morocco. They're already in Libya, as you know. If they do that, the flimsy fiction that Vichy France is a neutral country will disappear. And French North Africa will then be governed by the Nazis, full stop. At which point we American diplomats become enemy aliens, and who can say where that will lead. There's also the possibility that Franco might decide to come south in force—maybe even if the Nazis don't take over France. We are trying to prepare for either scenario by building anti-Vichy French and some unruly Arabs into a network of saboteurs and spies. If the Germans do come, they'll come from the east, so our network is supposed to blow up roadways and bridges and harass them in any way possible. Then once they're here—to make their lives miserable through sabotage and the usual tricks."

"Including spreading the exploding mule shit."

"Yes! Eddy told you about that, did he? Brilliant, no? I'd love to be there when the first German staff car hits the shit! *Mein Gott im Himmel! Ein Scheisse Landminen!* Anyway, we're also here to set up secret radio stations, because regular transmissions from our offices in Tangier and Casablanca are not secure, and we need to keep London informed of what's happening here. Things change so quickly that written messages sent in a diplomatic pouch may be too late."

"I've heard about those suitcase radio sets. Parasets? One of our sailors built a replica last year when we were tracking U-boats."

"Yes. The Parasets are very clever devices. So, all things considered, we've done pretty well building an organization. Our other job is to smuggle people out of here. Vichy passed a law saying that no European man from any of the belligerent countries could leave French North Africa. There must be hundreds or even a couple thousand such men here, and the Vichy-slash-Krauts don't want them going home or to England and joining up. The ones they've caught or rounded up have been put in camps in the desert. But others are still lurking around in the shadows, so we smuggle them out the best we can—along with our people who've been blown. It's a tricky business, because all the exits are watched by the Vichy police. The same goes for Spanish Morocco, which is especially difficult, because Tangier is a much better exit than, say, Casablanca. Closer to Gibraltar, obviously, and Tangier has an airport serving Europe. Casablanca doesn't."

"No? That's surprising."

"Maybe. But that's the situation."

"So you are busy."

"Busier than a two-peckered goat. It means, though, that we're watched pretty closely, because as I say, all of this stuff is illegal according to Vichy regulations. The Twelve Apostles have diplomatic status, but of course none of our agents do. Vichy enforces their regulations either to make the Nazis happy or because they are true believers. Doesn't much matter which. They're watching anyone they suspect of being one of our people. They have those direction-finding vehicles out and about, looking for our radios. They have plenty of agents and, I'm afraid, double agents sniffing everywhere. The local Moors have their own agenda and will take money from anyone and everyone and deliver information that may or may not be reliable. So while we use them, we don't especially trust them. All of which brings us to your mission.

"Frankly, it's going to be difficult, if not impossible, for you *personally* to get the information you want about the Sebou. I've been thinking about it and I can't see how you can do it. If you go up there and start sniffing around and asking locals about the channels and shipping, you're bound to come to the attention of the Vichy police or army."

"I was thinking that I might go as an assistant to the Twelve Apostle inspectors."

"Yes, I thought of that, too. We could whip up some credentials without any trouble. But I doubt that they'd buy it, and more importantly, your poking around up there could be a real threat to the security of the whole operation. The problem is, Port Lyautey has not been used as a depot for any of the imported aid. Casablanca and Tangier are much bigger ports and have better facilities for offloading and distribution. There'd be no reason to use Lyautey. None. If you suddenly appear and start asking questions about the depth of the channel, which has never been used to receive those shipments—and might not even be capable of it—somebody's going to wonder why, and then a smarter somebody is going to put two and two together and figure you're scouting for military reasons. And even worse, since no one would believe that Port Lyautey could be a *primary* military objective of any consequence, they would naturally assume that the main target is Casablanca or maybe Rabat, and that Lyautey is a subset of that. All of which would be perfectly true. What's more, looking at the bigger picture, the Krauts know as well as we do that Stalin is agitating for a second front. Two and two and two make six."

"But what if we said we were thinking of expanding our aid in such a way that would require additional ports, like Lyautey?"

"I thought of that, too, but it's more than a little thin. Another ship in either Casablanca or Tangier is not going to tax the facilities. Not only that, there are two smaller but serviceable Atlantic ports at Fedala and Safi."

"Not a very convincing story, then."

"No. When you're casting a fly to a trout, you should use something that at least looks like a bug he normally eats."

"Funny you should mention that. The week before I came down here I was fishing on the Test."

"Really? Well done! That's a great river. How'd you do?"

"Pretty well, I think. Well enough to understand your point about choosing the proper fly."

"And more to the point—not choosing the wrong one. These Vichy trout are suspicious and skittish buggers, and we'll only get one cast at them. Mess it up, and they'll go on the alert."

"Well, the sad story is, I just took up the sport a week ago. I'm not sure my casting is up to the challenge."

"Not to worry. I have an idea that I think might actually succeed. How would you feel about a little friendly kidnapping and smuggling? Sound interesting?"

"Up to a point."

"Ha! Good one. You've been talking to Eddy. But seriously, I think this idea could work."

"Does it involve a camel and a burnoose?"

"Don't worry. No camels or midnight rides in the desert."

"That sounds better. Do I have to wear a fez?"

"Optional. You should seriously consider it, though. After all, how many more chances will you have in this life to wear exotic native garb and be almost authentic? You wouldn't want to miss it. I'm sure you agree."

"Up to a point."

Chapter Ten

"So one day Hershel the *schnorrer* woke up feeling sickly," said Moshe, as we were driving back to the hotel. "He decided he should go to the doctor, and asked his rabbi who was the best doctor in the region. The rabbi recommended someone, but warned Hershel that this doctor was the most expensive physician for miles around. But Hershel went to him anyway, and when the doctor had examined Hershel and given him a costly drug, he presented Hershel with the bill, and Hershel said, 'I'm sorry, I have no money.' The doctor was shocked and said, 'I am well known as the most expensive physician in all the region. If you have no money, why did you come to me?' And Hershel said, 'When it comes to my good health, nothing is too expensive.'"

"I'm going to have to write these down," I said.

"Yes. For your memoirs. Where are we going?"

"You're the rabbi. You tell me."

"I meant right now, not metaphysically."

"Well, then, the hotel. I have time for a shower and brush-up, but I'll be meeting King again at Charlie's at seven. Out of curiosity, what's your duty with me? Any specific orders?" I pretty much knew the answer, but I was interested in what he knew about the assignment.

"Nothing specific, no. I'm to stay with you and drive you wherever you want to go for as long as you're here—which suggests to me that you are not here permanently."

"Who is?"

"Another metaphysical joke. Very good."

"Okay. So for the time being, you're working for me?"

"Yes, sir. As the Andrews trio so nicely put it, I'll be with you till apple blossom time."

"Well done, but it's the Andrews *Sisters*, and the line is 'I'll be with you *in* apple blossom time.' A small difference, but important."

"Thank you for the correction, Lieutenant. As a Talmudic scholar, I am a connoisseur of fine distinctions of language. Although I should say a *former* Talmudic scholar."

It was funny that Moshe should mention that song. It reminded me of one of the sailors on my ship. For some reason he couldn't stand the Andrews Sisters. He was on the fantail of the ship when the bomb hit, so we never found a trace of him. He wasn't the only one. I was going to miss him and all the rest of the men we lost that day. They were good guys. Every damned one of them. We all were.

Charlie's was packed again that evening. Cuddles guided Dave King and me to the same table we had had the night before. The band was playing "Love for Sale," but Amanda, aka Yvonne Dubonnet, had not appeared yet. I hadn't heard from her, but that was not surprising.

There was the usual racket of noise in the café, the usual fog of tobacco smoke, and nothing seemed out of the ordinary until about eight o'clock when two men, who were central-casting Gestapo agents, came walking in on either side of a blonde Valkyrie—a stunning statuesque woman wearing a black dress shimmering with sequins. She had long blonde hair and perfect Teutonic features, including a look of contempt for all things not her.

King watched her and grinned.

"This should be good."

"Who's that?"

"A visitor from another world. She forgot her spear and helmet, but otherwise she seems ready for action. She's a Mata Hari who comes down here now and then to put the Vichy boys through their paces. Name's Greta Wagner. Or so she says. I hope it's true. It's too good a joke not to be."

Cuddles guided the trio to a table not far from where we were sitting. They sat down and ordered champagne. The two men with Greta tried to look as though they were at ease and used to being with someone like her, but they couldn't pull it off. She may not have been their boss, but it certainly seemed that way. They looked around with exaggerated hauteur which showed very clearly that they were nervous about something. She on the other hand was not nervous about anything and gave the impression that she never had been and never would be. She pulled out a cigarette and, yes, inserted it into a twelve-inch gold-and-onyx holder. Her two assistants competed to see who could be the first to offer a light.

"I'll tell you a funny story about her," said King. "Last month she was in here on a night like this. The place was just as crowded and even a little more raucous. She and her two minders sat about where they are sitting now. They were drinking steadily and they got louder and louder and started singing dreadful German drinking songs, until finally people started shouting for them to shut up, but they wouldn't. Finally this Wagner woman stood up on a chair and in elegant although slightly slurred French, shouted, 'All you French pansies are a bunch of pathetic poufs! If you had anything between your legs you wouldn't have folded up like a Murphy bed! Ha, ha. And you dare to tell me to shut up. *Scheisse* to you!" And more along the same lines, and then she gave the crowd two fingers, which as you know is the European equivalent of the bird.

"Finally one of the Legionnaires in the room worked his way through the crowd, grabbed her by the front of her dress, dragged her off the chair, and popped her with a very fine right cross. She went down like she'd been filleted. Then the Legionnaire stood there daring her two henchmen to do something, but they didn't. They just picked her up and carried her out. She had a beautiful shiner for a week afterwards."

"You can push the French, but only so far."

"Only so far as Casablanca. Ha!"

"So what's her job here?"

"Who knows? She goes everywhere, and when the German generals or politicians come to town, she's their escort. So I guess her job is mostly horizontal. But she's well connected, no pun intended."

There had been a slight lull in the noise of the crowd as the three Germans entered, but now it resumed and the band started playing a song I didn't recognize as the lights were dimmed. And then Amanda stepped into the spotlight. I was glad to see her, glad she was still in town. She looked over at me and winked.

"I have a new song for you tonight," she said to the crowd, in her practiced smoky voice, as the band continued the first few bars of introduction. "It's about a soldier who meets his lover every evening. She waits for him each night under a lamppost. I see that our three friends from Germany have just joined us. I'm sure they will recognize it. It is very popular where they come from—and with their army. It's called 'Lili Marlene.'"

Then as the band moved into the main body of the song, she started to sing.

Vor der Kaserne,
Vor dem grossen Tor
Steht 'ne Laterne
Und steht sie noch davor
Dort wollen wir uns wiederseh'n
bei der Laterne wollen wir steh'n.

And to my utter surprise Amanda's voice was, if not beautiful, then beautifully suited to this sentimental song that would go on to be popular, absurdly, with all the armies of the Western war. Marlene Dietrich would sing it, Edith Piaf would sing it, Vera Lynn would sing it. Armies on both sides would sing along. It was so thoroughly sentimental, such a complete weeper, that no one listening to it that night, or, I suppose, any other night during this wretched war, could hold back at least a little tightening of the throat. Future generations would probably scorn, but only because they would not have been there. But we were.

As Amanda sang the German lyrics, the crowd in Charlie's gradually became silent and listened, for she was singing the story of the universal soldier who missed his girl and who wondered if he would ever see her again—whether he would ever return, and, if he did, whether she would still be there. If there was anything the human race had in common, it was that everyone had had that feeling, or one very like it, at some point in their lives. Or at the very least, they could understand it. Of course it was wartime and that brought the feeling closer to the surface, and made the dangers and likelihood of a sad ending that much more likely. And when Amanda came to the last verse, she changed to English ...

If harm should come to me,
who will stand at the lamppost with you, Lili Marlene,
with you, Lili Marlene?
From the quiet place out of the earthly ground,
I am lifted as in a dream to your loving lips.
When the evening mist swirls in, I will be standing at the
    lamplight,
as before, Lili Marlene,
as before, Lili Marlene.

On the page the words may look a little soppy or pathetic, but when married to the music they became something else again. And it occurred to me that a song was itself a different form—not just words set to music or music sprinkled with words, but a combination that made it into something else. As the phrase goes, something more than the sum of its parts. I would have to ask my friend Hobey, the writer, what he thought about that. He liked to use music references in his stories, so he might agree. Not that anyone read his stories anymore.

When Amanda finished, for a moment there was only silence in Charlie's. Then the applause broke out and shouts of *Encore!* and whistles, but Amanda was alive to the old showbiz saying of leaving them wanting more, and she merely bowed regally and stepped out of the spotlight and down from the stage and came over and sat down with me and King. For one of the few times since I'd known her she seemed totally without artifice, as though the song had touched her, too, the way that it had touched everyone, or almost everyone, in Charlie's. The only other times I had seen her that way, we were in bed together without our clothes. This was almost as good.

"That was lovely, Amanda," I said, sincerely.

"Yes," said King. "Worthy of a Parisian cabaret. More than that, really."

"Thank you, darlings. Are you surprised?"

"A bit."

"Good. Now, darling David, would you mind if I whispered something of a private nature in Riley's ear?"

"No, of course not. I am a gentleman above all."

"I know." She leaned close to me and said, "I have to get out of this town, and I need your help."

"What?"

"It's that woman. That Nazi bitch, Wagner. I can't say anything more about it here. I'll come to your room tonight. Okay? I was going to anyway, you know."

94

"Yes, of course."

"Thank you, darling. I have to go now. I will wait for you at the hotel. In your room."

"How will you get in?

She rolled her eyes and smiled, as if to say, "Surely you jest."

"Don't leave here for a while," she said. "People will catch on, if you do."

Then she left, with people still applauding her.

"What was that about?" said King.

"She's in some kind of trouble."

"Oh. That's hardly surprising. I'm sure you'll keep in mind what I said about her."

"Up to a point."

"Eh?"

"Just kidding."

Chapter Eleven

Earlier that day David King and I had developed a plan. It was his idea, but I liked it. More or less. At least I liked it better than anything I could have come up with.

"We've agreed, I think, that it's no good, your going up to the Sebou and Port Lyautey and sniffing around," said King.

"Yes. Two reasons. Ineffective, and potentially a risk to the security of the coming operation. Either one cancels the idea."

"Right. But there's a man we know, or at least we're aware of, who certainly can help us if we can persuade him to do it. A former river pilot of that very river. As a navy man you will understand the significance of that."

"Yes. I was discussing this situation with Bunny and he reminded me of Dr. Johnson's quote about two kinds of knowledge."

"Good. The old boy was right—Johnson, I mean. Well, this fellow's our second kind. His name is Jean-Loup Marcel."

"Jean-Loup? Means 'John Wolf.' Funny name."

"Yes. Unfortunately, he does not live up to the dashing style of his name. He is a rather timorous character who had a moderately bad time with the Vichy police last year and has gone to ground here, more like a hedgehog than a wolf."

"If he's a hedgehog, he knows the one very big thing."

"Yes—how to preserve himself—and he has that lesson down to a tee . . . But he knows the river, and I suggest that we snatch him from his hole and spirit him away to London, where he can explain the vagaries of the river and earn a medal doing so."

"Why London? Why not just Gibraltar?"

"London is where the planning brass are. There's nothing of that nature in Gib. Not yet, anyway. Besides, once you're out of Morocco there's no reason not to go all the way to London. Just as easy, really. And much more secure. So? What do you think?"

"It sounds like a good plan. Certainly better than my lurking on the riverbank with a lead line trying to figure depths."

"Good. Consider it your next assignment."

"Does he speak English? I took a two-week crash course in French in London, but I'm not sure I'm up to negotiations."

"Yes, he does. God knows where he picked it up. But he's fluent enough for our purposes." He smiled as if to say, *Give us a little credit for knowing what we're doing.* "We wouldn't have selected you for this job, otherwise."

"No, I suppose not. Where is he?"

"We don't really know, for sure. Somewhere in Casablanca, most likely in the native quarter. The medina. But we'll find out. We've been keeping very discreet eyes on him for the past year, just for this sort of venture. Nothing obvious. We don't want him to fly away. He moves around a lot, but always within a small radius, and always within the medina. We lose him for a while, but then he bobs back to the surface."

"Once we get him, then what? A ship leaving Casablanca?"

"I wish it could be that simple. But it isn't. The Vichy police and the Gestapo have all the French ports pretty well sewed up tight. Remember I mentioned earlier that part of our job is smuggling our people out of here? Well, we do it by taking them to Tangier and flying them out from there. The Spanish police are much less zealous—and more easily bribed. They really don't have a horse in this race, although they are sympathetic to the Nazis, of course. But the average Spanish cop doesn't have the Gestapo breathing beer fumes down his neck the way the Vichy boys do. It's much safer to go through Tangier. But . . ."

"There is always a *but*."

"Yes. In this case the *but* is the difficulty of getting people *to* Tangier—through the mobile roadblocks of the Vichy police, across the border, and into the city. Once there, it's not too bad. We can arrange the travel through Eddy's people up there. Either a fast boat across to Gib and then a plane to London, or a plane to Lisbon and then on to London."

"Do I babysit him all the way?"

"Yes. As I said, he's a very nervous guy who'd be perfectly capable of getting off somewhere along the route and disappearing."

"Okay. As a matter of curiosity, why is he so shy?"

"Well, last year the Vichy police here grabbed him for having Gaullist sympathies. They figured he was up to something, and that was enough. They sent him up to Vichy France for trial and let him languish in a jail cell for a couple of months before they got around to it. In the end, they had no real evidence against him—primarily because he had never done anything and didn't really know de Gaulle from Napoleon—a comparison that exists only in de Gaulle's fevered imagination, I might say. And so they let him go and sent him back to Morocco. But the experience was enough for him, and he quit his job as a river pilot and came to Casablanca and more or less went to ground."

"How does he live?"

"Ah, well, you won't be surprised to hear that there's plenty of opportunity for petty crime and not-so-petty crime in a city like this. We figure he is doing enough to keep body and soul together somehow. Only barely. But nothing that's aroused the interest of the police. They tend to avoid the medina anyway, which is the reason he's holed up in there. All of that is good, obviously. We'd rather no one was watching him, except us, and as far as we can tell, no one is."

"What's his incentive to work for us?"

"The usual."

"Money."

"Yes. I suppose it's theoretically possible that he really does have Free French sympathies and that he just did a good job of hiding them from the police. Maybe in that case he'll tell himself he's doing it for France. But I doubt it. He certainly has never been a part of the network we have built—and continue to build. Never approached us to volunteer for anything."

"Have we approached him?

"No. As I suggested, we have sort of been saving him for this kind of operation. So it'll be about money. Tell him we have a lot of it and would like to give him some. Don't worry about a budget. Promise whatever you think will get the job done. But tell him that he'll have to wait until you and he get to London before he gets the bulk of the cash. Tell him once he gets to London he'll be given a prince's ransom, and he can buy a place in Mayfair or Belgravia and have tea with the King on Tuesdays."

"Will we deliver?" It made me a trifle squeamish to offer this little guy something, knowing that we'd back out when he'd done what we wanted. This was war, of course, and apparently there were no rules. Still . . .

"Yes. But be sensible. Nothing on the order of the Blue Water diamond. And I was kidding about Mayfair. Bear in mind that this guy is living hand to mouth by picking pockets and probably pimping. How is that for alliteration?"

"He'll want something up front, though."

"Yes. You can give him a down payment. Let me know how much you need after you've got him hooked. Call me here and whisper a number, and you'll have the cash within mere minutes. Then we'll go from there."

"What if he says no?"

"In that case, it's your job to show him the error of his ways. We have some very good stuff that will knock a midsize elephant out for eight hours. A second dose gives you another eight, and so on. Very reliable. More than enough time for a trip to Tangier and beyond. If it comes to that, give him a shot and just pack up him in your old kit bag and smile, smile, smile. You've heard that song, I assume."

"Yes. Not one of my favorites, but I understand the point. Worst case, we kidnap him."

"Yes. He'll feel better about things when he wakes up at the Dorchester and finds he can order room service. Not that the food is any good there, especially these days."

"How do we get to Tangier?"

"Well, there are several possible ways, all of which are obvious, unfortunately. We could try using a ship or boat of some kind and leave from some remote spot on the coast. But that's dangerous and slow. There's a lot of smuggling going on all along the coast. *Quelle surprise!* The French customs inspectors and the navy have patrol boats out and about constantly. You'd be sure to be spotted and searched, and that would be that. We could put you on the train that runs from here to Tangier—and right through Port Lyautey, by the way—but we've had mixed results sending refugees by train. The damned problem with trains is that there's nowhere to go if you're spotted. You can't jump off a speeding express, so you're left dodging in and out of compartments, and you're sure to be caught eventually. So, we've found that the best way to smuggle someone out is by car. We'll rig up some sort of convincing-looking trailer. Something used to carry extra gas tanks. The French know as well as we do that there aren't any Esso stations along the road, so people routinely carry gas cans in little trailers. It's worked before. It's really all just a matter of talking your way past the roadblocks. And you'll have diplomatic papers. As long as our friend stays hidden in the trailer, you'll be fine."

"What if they search the trailer and find him?"

"Then you'll have a choice to make. Use the thirty-eight you carry, or go off to jail."

"Shoot a couple of our French allies?"

"They're not our allies, yet. And if the French decide to get fussy about this coming amphibious operation, we'll be shooting a lot more of them. That question is still hovering over all the planning, and it probably will right up to the day we land."

"They may fight. Oppose the landings."

"Very possibly. You know what de Gaulle says about his countrymen? *How can anyone govern a nation that has two hundred and forty-six kinds of cheese?* It's his only known witticism and says a lot about the political situation here and the uncertainty we're facing—and will continue to face. Considered in that context, I wouldn't worry overmuch about shooting a few border guards. They probably have mothers somewhere, but don't let that bother you. But do it discreetly, if you have to."

"What about the car?"

"Use the one you came in. Moshe can drive. It will look more official, if you don't drive yourself. Besides, he regularly goes back and forth on that road. It's possible someone—maybe a few of the border sentries—will recognize him as a Consulate employee."

"Is Moshe completely reliable?"

"He's a Jew running from the Nazis with a promise of a trip to the United States, if he's a good boy. That's as close to completely reliable as we get in this business."

"A very large carrot."

"Yes. And he's running just ahead of a very large stick."

"He sweats at the roadblocks and border."

"I don't blame him. I would too, in his shoes."

"Eddy told me not to trust anyone, though."

"Yes. Well, there's always that to think about."

"How should I go about finding this Jean-Loup?"

"Oh, don't worry about that. We'll find him for you. If we could, we'd bring him in, but he's a cagey fellow. He'll be on the alert—for the wrong reasons. He'll think the police are after him for whatever he's doing. But that doesn't matter much. He'll still be very wary. We'll locate him for you, but you have to make the snatch. You're a new face, you see? He's somewhere in the bowels of the medina. And those people know all of us. You're a different story."

"Is that why I was sent here?"

"Well, perhaps it's one reason."

"What are the other reasons?"

"I don't know. Give me some time, and I'll think of them. But I think it's safe to say that the lower-level Vichy and Gestapo agents don't know you yet. When we locate Jean-Loup, you should be able to go there, make the deal, and get him out of there in one fell swoop."

"What do I tell him about the mission?"

"Not much. Just that it involves a trip to Tangier, that it's a perfectly safe courier-type operation."

"But won't he wonder why he of all people is being recruited?"

"Let him wonder. He probably won't believe anything you tell him, but he'll believe the cash. That's all he needs to know and all he's going to know, until he meets the planners in London."

"And if he refuses, I stick him with the sweet-dreams needle and bundle him away in the car."

"Yes. Moshe will assist, if you need him. But this Jean-Loup is a bantamweight and looks consumptive. Like a starving Left Bank poet. I doubt he'd give you any trouble, if it comes to a struggle. I don't think it will. As I said, the Vichy people gave him a rough time. He may well convince himself that taking a large sum of money while getting some sort of revenge is nice compensation."

"Okay."

"So, are we agreed on the basics?"

"Agreed."

"Good. There's one more thing I must tell you. From this moment on, you must never again utter the words 'Sebou River' or 'Port Lyautey.' Not to Amanda, not to Moshe, not even to me. No one. Forget that you ever heard of these places. I mean that quite literally. Absolutely. Never speak their names. All right? Consider them top-secret. And consider that an order."

King was deadly serious.

"Yes, sir. Even Jean-Loup?"

"Especially Jean-Loup. *Comprenez-vous?*"

"*Absolument.*"

"Well, then, what do you say to another evening at Charlie's? Meet you there at seven?"

"Yes."

So that was the plan.

And that evening, just after Amanda had sung "Lili Marlene," whispered in my ear, and left, King and I had sat at the table at Charlie's and had a few drinks, just like a couple of guys relaxing after a day at the office.

Every once in a while I'd look up and see the Valkyrie staring at me. For a nice-looking woman, she was very unattractive, but I had noticed before that the difference between beauty and ugliness is not always that great. I mean, Mona Lisa? Really? And I'd seen some actresses in Hollywood who looked like a bad memory, until they got their makeup and camera lighting just right—at which point they turned into heart-stoppers. Anyway, this woman's unattractiveness was more in her expression than her features. The way she glared at us, she looked like Grendel's mother in bright red lipstick and a platinum wig. She should cut back a little on the mascara, too. And she might consider passing on the starchy foods for a while, although I think the Germans liked their women husky.

Her two minders, as Dave King called them, also kept an eye on us, as though trying to prove to her that they were worth their pay envelopes. They were trying to look sinister, but they looked like twerps to me.

After about an hour or so, they left.

"Probably going back to the hotel. They're at the Anfa, too. In fact, the entire German Armistice Committee stays there, along with their hangers-on. It's something to keep in mind, if you hadn't already thought of it."

I hadn't, but I would now.

"I suppose it's okay to leave now. I imagine Amanda's managed to lose her shadows."

"Probably, but it doesn't matter. Everyone knows who's doing who around here. As a former Harvard man, I should say who's doing 'whom.' But it always sounds a little prissy. So—as P. G. Wodehouse might say, 'Heaven speed your wooing.' I'm green with envy when I think of your immediate future."

"You mean my adventure à la Jean-Loup?"

"That, too. But I was thinking more along the lines of the next few hours. I'll see you tomorrow. By mid-morning I expect we'll have some word about where our hedgehog is burrowed. If you can think of anything else overnight, we can talk about it in the morning. The phone at my villa is secure, we think, but even so, it would be best to talk discreetly. No names. No real ones, I mean."

"Sounds good."

"Tell 'Yvonne' I said *Bonsoir*."

Chapter Twelve

Amanda was in my room when I returned. I didn't ask how she'd gotten in.

"Darling," she said, with an imitation look of longing. "I've been so terribly lonely waiting for you."

"And who could blame you."

"Did you get everything settled with King?"

"What do you mean?"

"Oh, never mind. You really are horrible, and I may begin to hate you. But only after you've done me a favor."

"Is that what they're calling it these days? You Brits used to call it 'shagging,' but I suppose 'doing me a favor' is more polite."

"Darling, you are too tiresome. But I forgive you, for two reasons."

"What's the other one?"

"I need your help."

"So you said. Well?"

"It's . . . a little embarrassing."

"I'm shocked."

"Yes, well, you might actually be, when I tell you all."

"I'll be shocked if you *do* tell me all—about anything, ever. But of course I won't be able to know whether you have or not. It's a kind of philosophical problem. A 'What Is Reality' sort of thing."

"Don't be obscure. You saw that horrid Nazi woman."

"Yes. The three Rhine maidens rolled into one."

"Yes. And . . . well . . . I don't know how to say this, really."

She actually seemed to blush.

"Give truth a try."

"You have to believe that I've never done anything like that before."

And she was actually blushing. Her lovely throat was suddenly blotchy and red.

"You're kidding! You and her?"

"Yes. But only just the once. I came home from a show at Charlie's, and it was late, and I'd had quite a lot to drink. As I was undressing there was a knock at the door and I asked who it was, and she said something about the Vichy police, so I opened the door and there she stood in a flimsy negligee holding a bottle of champagne and two glasses, and she said, 'May I come in?' Well, what was I supposed to do?"

"Was it good champagne?"

"Oh, I don't know. You know I don't know anything about wine. I like all kinds."

"Yes, you upper-class English girls only learn what's done and what's not done. You told me. So, does what happened next fall into the 'Done' category? Is it the sort of thing that goes on in girls' boarding schools?"

"Well . . . it's not unheard of. But I had never done anything like that before. Do you believe me?"

"Does it matter? If it does, then, yes, I believe you utterly and with no reservations. How was it?"

"Well, I was the passive one, of course, so when I closed my eyes like Mrs. Lloyd George and thought of England, it was not unlike some things I had known before, with one or two men. Including you, darling. Of course, there were some differences, even with my eyes closed."

"I'm pleased to hear it."

"But she is an odious woman. She hadn't shaved under her arms."

"*That* was what bothered you?"

"Yes, among many, many other things. Her breath was not to be believed. The next day, I tried to tell her that I was drunk and that I had never done those things before and didn't really want to do them again, but she wouldn't take no for an answer. Did you see the way she was glaring at you at Charlie's?"

"Yes. I assumed she was thinking I was dashingly handsome and debonair."

"Well, you are that, of course, darling. But she was thinking that you're some sort of rival. Which you are, you know."

"That's a first for me—rival to a Nazi Sappho."

"Anyway, I wouldn't think anything of the whole matter, except that it was too shame-making, as the Bright Young Things used to say. The problem is, she's some sort of Gestapo queen. She can make life very difficult for me, and she will, absolutely."

"Hell hath no fury like a woman scorned by another woman."

"Right. When I told her I didn't want to play the little Dutch boy anymore, she threatened me in no uncertain terms."

"Little Dutch boy?"

"You know that story. Don't be coy, darling. But I have to get out of town. There's nothing here for me anyway, not really, and since you're in the Consulate now and can move around fairly easily, and even have a car, I was hoping you could whisk me off to Tangier. It's not that far a drive, and if we left early in the morning, we could do it easily in a day, and you could be back by evening. I can get a plane to Lisbon from there and put this whole nightmare behind me. Will you please be my knight in shining armor and spirit me away like Lochinvar or Lancelot or whoever it was that swooped in and threw his girl over his pommel and rode off? Will you, darling?"

"I'll see what I can do."

"That's all I ask. One way or the other I'm getting out of this town, and I'd much rather it be with you than any other way."

"So would I."

"Oh, good. Maybe we could have a sort of honeymoon in Tangier."

"Would we have to get married first?"

"Of course not." She paused and looked at me. "You weren't serious . . . for just a second I thought . . ."

"My darling, with you I am never serious."

"I'm glad. It's much more civilized that way. I don't want to be married again, ever. And now, shall we order room service before or after?"

"After."

"Mmm, I'm glad you said that. That's what I want, too, even though our afters usually take such a long, lovely time coming."

I didn't believe much, if anything, of her story. But I believed the way she was taking off her dress and all the rest of her silky things. And I believed the way she stretched her naked body languorously against mine. And I believed her perfume and the way she kissed. That was enough belief for the time being.

I figured as long as she thought there was a chance I'd give her a ride out of there, she wouldn't steal my wallet and sneak out while I was asleep. And there would come a time later when I would have to fall asleep. But not for the next couple of hours.

In the morning I would call Dave King and see what he thought about this new wrinkle. There was certainly more going on here than I could know, but I had a feeling King might have a clue about what it was, and if there was a rat lurking somewhere, he'd sniff it.

And then I thought of de Gaulle's two hundred and forty-six kinds of cheese—which meant two hundred and forty-six kinds of bait for a rat trap. If I was meant to be one of them—in other words, a wedge of bait—I hoped at least it would be smooth, sophisticated, and robust, with no unpleasant odor.

"By the way, Amanda, has anyone ever told you that you have the most intoxicating scent?"

"No. No one. I'm glad you're the first."

"Of course."

"So, darling, would you like me to show you how to play the little Dutch boy?"

"I don't know. It sounds like I don't have the proper equipment."

"*Au contraire*, darling. You're just right for the way I want to play it. My way is a departure from the rules."

"That figures."

Chapter Thirteen

THE NEXT MORNING, IT WAS THE REPRISE OF THE OLD BLUES SONG. I was just as glad she was gone. She wouldn't have gone far, and I had things to do. And my wallet was still on the dresser.

I called King and made a date to get together with him at his villa at ten o'clock. I thought that would be better than discussing Amanda over the phone. I had my doubts about the security of the phone lines.

Just before ten, Moshe pulled up outside the hotel. King had apparently told him to pick me up. The old Chevy was pulling a small wooden trailer. It had a peaked roof over it and looked a lot like a doghouse on two wheels. It was maybe four feet long and three feet wide.

"What's this?" I asked, even though I knew.

"Mr. King told me to attach it. It is something we use to carry spare cans of petrol, when we are going on a trip of some kind. I assume that we are going on a trip of some kind."

"Talmudic deduction."

"Yes. That, and the fact that Mr. King told me about it."

King had evidently located Jean-Loup. Events were moving fast.

We drove to King's villa. Moshe waited in the car while I went inside.

"Found him?" I said.

"Yes. The trailer gave it away, I suppose. As we suspected, he's in the medina in a shabby one-room apartment above a hashish store. Very sinister neighborhood. The snatch is best done in daylight in that neighborhood—for the safety of the snatchers, rather than the snatchee."

"We go today?"

"Yes. The sooner, the better. I've put together a package of things you'll need. Here's a case containing three hypodermic needles with the sleepytime stuff already loaded. That will give him twenty-four hours of peaceful dreams, if you decide to use it. Here's a glass vial for you, personally. In the vial are three capsules—Benzedrine, in case you need to stay awake for twenty-four hours or so; a Mickey Finn, in case you want to spike someone's drink; and a cyanide capsule in case you get captured. Try not to get them confused. The cyanide is the brown one. I'm told it's painless and works extremely fast."

"Suddenly the romance of this adventure is evaporating."

"Well, it's just a precaution. We all carry them around. Standard-issue. It will make you feel you're one of the OSS boys. Jack Armstrong, Secret Agent. I don't know anyone who's actually used any of the stuff. Or rather, seen it used, since in the case of the cyanide, personal testimonials are unlikely."

"I feel better now. Speaking of romantic adventures, our friend Amanda asked me to help her escape to Tangier. She's got herself mixed up with a Gestapo agent who will not take *nein* for an answer."

"Do you believe her?"

"Not entirely. But it could be true. Some of it is certainly true."

"Who's the swain?"

"The Valkyrie."

"Really? I had no idea Amanda was so . . . encyclopedic."

"It was a mistake committed under the influence of champagne. Now she wants to get out of here and up to Tangier to catch a flight to Lisbon. But the real question is—would taking her along jeopardize the safety of the mission? Under normal circumstances, I would be happy to help her out."

"Yes, as would I. I like her, as a matter of fact. She's as phony as the proverbial three-dollar bill, but I don't think there's anything really wrong about her. I mean, she takes a few bucks from us to spread some minor lies, and I'm sure she does the same for Vichy. But I don't think there's much more to her than that."

"You've checked?"

"Of course we have. She's harmless. The only danger she poses is talking about things she's overheard and probably doesn't understand. That's why it's critical to say nothing of interest when you're with her. That's a good rule for when you're with *anyone*, for that matter. Common sense."

I was more than a little relieved to hear it. Surprisingly so.

"So what do you think? Shall I give her a ride?"

"I'm sure it would be okay. You could make a case that taking her even adds to the appearance of an innocent trip. Very domestic. Family outing. Husband, wife . . . rabbi. A typical ménage."

"Not in Ohio. Or even Hollywood, for that matter."

"Just joking. But the key is, no one aside from you knows what this trip is all about, anyway. Moshe's just the driver. Jean-Loup will know he's been hired, but he won't know for what."

"He may well be asleep in the trailer."

"Asleep or awake, he'll definitely be in the trailer. So even if you were all arrested for some strange reason, they could question all three of the others and get nothing."

"Won't they be suspicious, if they find Jean-Loup hiding back there?"

"They probably won't search the trailer. Those things are common on the roads, and there are some gas cans in there to add to the illusion. But if they do happen to find him, just tell them he's not really hiding. He's a random hitchhiker you picked up. He had to sit back there, because there was no room in the car, or because he smelled like a goat."

"What about me?"

"You don't smell like a goat."

"Good to know. But is there anything special about my cover story?"

"No. You simply play the Consulate card. It's entirely legitimate. The other three don't know anything and you are a diplomat of a recognized foreign nation with your papers entirely in order. An official naval attaché. Just demand your release. Be firm, but not imperious or obnoxious. They'll be suspicious of bluster, since you're not a Kraut. Chances are, you'll be on your way again in no time."

"No need for the cyanide pill?"

"Too drastic. Anyone who stops you will just be run-of-the-mill Vichy cops or native troops. No Gestapo goons. They like to stay in the city. The desert is too hot for leather trench coats."

"All right. Now what are the next steps with Jean-Loup?"

"I have everything ready for you. In your package are ten thousand dollars in twenties. He'll be happy that they're dollars and not any other kind of European currency."

"Even Reichsmarks?"

"In a couple of years the Reichsmarks won't be good for anything but blowing your nose. There won't even be a Reich."

"Jean-Loup won't know that."

"No. Not as certainly as we do. But he'll have considered it. He'll want dollars. It's the currency of all black markets in Morocco—and, I suspect, all black markets everywhere. Something all Americans should be proud of, eh? There are travel papers for him in the package, too. Nothing fancy. He's just a peasant going north to visit his aged mother. Since he was once picked up by the Vichy cops, they'll have a record of his name, so we've given him a *nom de guerre*—Marcel Proust."

"The guy who made a big deal out of eating a cookie?"

"The same. There's not a Vichy cop in all of Morocco who'll know that name. And there'll certainly be no problem with the native troops. Most of them can't read. The ones who can wouldn't like Proust. I mean, who does? Okay?"

"Yes."

"Moshe has his documents—all legit—and we can assume that Amanda has hers—a transit visa and an exit visa for Lisbon."

"Are you sure?"

"We're talking about Amanda, aren't we? But I'd make sure before you leave."

"I see your point. And I suppose even if she doesn't have an exit visa, she could hole up in Tangier until she gets one, one way or the other."

"She's a big girl."

"Yes. So . . . how much of the ten thousand should I offer?"

"Start with a thousand, and if he bites—which he may very well do—pocket the rest for expenses."

"A gangster friend of mine in Hollywood always says, 'When the girl says yes, stop talking and keep the jewelry in your pocket.'"

"Words to live by."

"Out of curiosity—is it real money? That same gangster refers to phony money as 'fugazi.'"

"Real? Up to a point. It certainly appears to be, although I'm no expert. Put it this way—Jean-Loup will be able to spend it in places he frequents, so what's the difference? Keep your receipts for expenses. The bean counters in London will be sure to check, and they'll expect you to turn over any leftover cash."

"Even if it's . . . fugazi?"

"That's why they're bean counters. Of course, they'll have to take your word for the amount you gave Jean-Loup. But that's their problem. I'm not going to worry about it."

"I've been told I have an honest face."

"Really? I'm surprised. Now, here's the address of Jean-Loup's hole. Moshe can find it without any trouble. He's been briefed and knows how to get there and what to do, if you need help. Any questions?"

"Just one. To be absolutely clear—I am not to tell Jean-Loup what he's being hired to do, nor even hint at it. Just that it's a routine and safe job that will involve a little travel—albeit involving some secrecy."

"Yes, he'll know you're an American, and he'll know this has something to do with the war. He may suspect what the job's about. He'll be reluctant, until you've offered him more cash today than he's been able to steal in the last twelve months—with the promise of much more to come, once you're out of the country. That's all he'll need to know, and he'll be satisfied with that, most likely. If not, sweet dreams, and Moshe will help you carry the sleeping beauty to the trailer."

"What are the odds of having to do that?"

"Fifty-fifty, I'd say. As I said before, he tends toward the timorous end of the animal spectrum."

"Okay. I think that's it."

"Good. Well, then, anchors aweigh. I hope we meet again sometime."

"I do, too. And thanks."

"One last thing. I have a present for you. A little something to remember us by."

It was a fez.

"Gee, thanks, again. I've always wanted one of these."

"Like socks at Christmas? Who says dreams don't come true. Well, as Moshe would say, wear it in good health. It will look very dashing on Piccadilly. Tell Amanda so long for me, and thanks for the memories. Good luck."

Moshe was waiting, as expected.

"You know what we're doing?"

"Yes, sir. Mr. King gave me the general outlines."

"Well, before we pick up the passenger for the trailer, we've got to make a quick stop back at the hotel. I need to get my things together, and we'll have a last-minute, unexpected guest passenger. I suppose there's a *schnorrer* joke about people popping up unexpectedly."

"Yes, there is. But I have forgotten it."

"Then how can you be sure there is one?"

"Ah! Another philosophical dilemma. Much like the old yeshiva question—if a man tells a joke and no one hears it, is it a joke?"

We hurried back to the Anfa Hotel, and Moshe found a place to wait near the front. I ran upstairs and knocked on Amanda's door. Luckily, she was in, and even up and dressed for the day.

"Darling! This is a pleasant surprise. But it's so early. You *are* impetuous this morning. I'm flattered."

"Pack your bags, honey, if you want a ride to Tangier. We leave in ten minutes. I've got to get my stuff together, but I'll be back for you in just a minute. Okay? Yes or no. I can't wait for you to write in your diary."

"Yes. I'll be ready."

I went to my room and got my few things together. I forgot to ask King about wearing my uniform. Maybe it would be better cover than the suit I had on, but maybe not. I decided against it, threw my things in my navy duffel, big enough to pack a small piano, and hurried back to Amanda's room.

"Ready?"

"Yes," she said. "But darling, there's a slight problem."

"Another shock."

"It's only a little one. You see, I haven't actually paid my hotel bill. And I'm a little short."

"I only get a lieutenant's pay."

"I'm not asking you for money. But you're sweet to offer. All you need to do is carry my suitcase down with your things. If I walk through the lobby with it, they might think I was trying to get away without paying."

"People can be suspicious."

"I know. Will you do that for me, darling? Then I can meet you out front maybe five minutes later. They won't say anything if I'm just coming and going as usual."

"All right. We'll be in a green Chevrolet with a doghouse trailer, across the street. Don't forget to look both ways before you cross."

"Thank you, darling. That will give me just enough time to put on the rest of my makeup. I want to look nice for you."

"You look beautiful just the way you are."

And that was true. It was a good thing. Would I have left her there otherwise? Probably. After all, she was in no danger except from the embraces of a hairy Valkyrie with halitosis.

On the other hand, it was just possible there was something else going on. You never could tell with Amanda. There was only one thing she was ever sincere about, and in that case she really had no control over it, or herself. It just came naturally, after twenty minutes or so.

"Here," I said. "Put this in your purse."

It was my snub-nosed .38 Special.

"What for?"

"Just in case."

She pushed the barrel-release button on the side below the hammer and the barrel dropped open. She knew what she was doing.

"There are only five bullets."

"I always keep the hammer closed on an empty chamber. That way if you drop it, it won't go off. Besides, if you need more than five shots, you're in trouble. Having a sixth probably wouldn't matter."

I didn't think it would be gentlemanly of me to remind her that, when she'd shot her husband, by accident, she'd only needed one.

"What about you? Won't you need it?"

"I have another one. Now hurry up, please."

My bill was sent to the Consulate automatically, so there was no reason to stop at the checkout desk.

I shouldered my duffel and picked up Amanda's one suitcase, which was surprisingly light, and took the elevator to the main floor. A minute later and I was in the front seat of the Chevy.

"We have to wait for the mystery guest, but only a few minutes."

"I remembered the joke," said Moshe.

"Let's hear it."

"Hershel the *schnorrer* goes to one of his usual benefactors, but this time he has a young man with him. He rings the bell and the benefactor looks at Hershel, sorrowfully, of course. Who likes to open the door and see a *schnorrer*? Anyway, the benefactor asks Hershel who the young man is, and Hershel says, 'It's my son-in-law. I'm bringing him into the business.'"

"Only marginally relevant, Moshe."

"Maybe it's not the one I remembered."

Chapter Fourteen

As it turned out, Jean-Loup *did* smell like a goat, and we were glad to have the trailer available, for that reason alone.

His shabby room was in a shabby neighborhood, dark and sinister, as we expected. Almost a cliché, which Hollywood would have easily sanitized and turned into Omar Khayyam-ville, but which would have taken a good deal more work, in reality. The streets were narrow, dusty, and dirty, but fortunately they were just wide enough for the Chevy. Moshe had to go slowly to let the pedestrians and loungers and various domestic animals move out of the way. People sat in their doorways and glowered at us as we crept by. Not all of them, though. A few street merchants noticed Amanda in the backseat and rushed to the window to offer different items of Moorish junk. Here and there we would come to a wider spot in the road where there was a kind of square. Street vendors were selling kebabs cooking over smoking grills. It smelled pretty good. Then we'd creep back into the narrow alleys. It took thirty minutes or so to get to Jean-Loup's burrow.

"This is not a very nice neighborhood," said Amanda.

"We won't be here long. Just long enough to pick up a passenger."

"Oh, dear. Will he have to sit back here with me?"

"To be determined. But this guy's the reason we're going to Tangier. You can change your mind about going along, if you like. We'll drop you back at the hotel."

"No, darling. Thank you. I've checked out, remember?"

Jean-Loup's two-story apartment building seemed to be sagging a little to the side. Like almost all the buildings in the medina, it was made of bricks that were plastered over. It had started life painted white, but the years had dulled its luster, unlike what they had done to Cleopatra. The hashish store on the main floor was curtained and dark, but when we pulled up, a head poked out from the strands of beads that served as the doorway cover. The head was wearing a fez like mine, except that his was not new, and mine had no moth holes. When he saw the car and the dashing young fellow in the white linen diplomat's suit, he disappeared back into the gloom. The stairs to Jean-Loup's apartment were on the outside, on the side of the building.

"Do you happen to know if there's a back exit to this place?"

"I do, because I checked, and there is not," said Moshe.

"Good. Wait here, and if our man tries to make a break for it, don't let him."

"I believe it is proper to say aye, aye when given a naval order."

"Yes. I won't be too long."

"I hope not," said Amanda.

"Do you want your case—with the medical devices?" said Moshe, who had obviously been well briefed.

"Yes. Good idea. Thanks for reminding me."

I went up the staircase and knocked on the door. It opened slightly and a pair of beady, bloodshot eyes looked out. The face might have belonged to Peter Lorre, a few decades in the future.

"Oui?"

"Jean-Loup Marcel?"

"*Peut-être.*" Which meant, *Perhaps.* "*Qui êtes-vous?*"

"*Un ami.*"

"A friend I do not know and have never seen before? This is something rare."

"So is a friend with money, I imagine. May I come in? I have something of value to offer you."

"Another rarity. A miracle, even." Jean-Loup regarded me suspiciously, but he could see that I was clean and well-dressed, so that set me apart from the people he usually dealt with, many of whom weren't even remotely friendly. "Well, *entrez, s'il vous plaît.*"

He opened the door and I went into a room that was remarkable in its disorder and shabbiness. The petty crime business was not all that good, apparently. Either that, or Jean-Loup was not any good at it. There were a few pieces of collapsed furniture scattered around— an ancient sofa that had a swayback like a twenty-year-old horse, a threadbare carpet that might have been decent-looking if it had been cleaned. A rough wooden table with the remains of the week's dishes, piled up and attracting flies.

Jean-Loup himself was a small, squat man in a soiled white shirt and black baggy pants held up by suspenders. He wore a blue beret, perhaps as a way of asserting his French-ness. He needed a shave, and he had the stereotypical cigarette butt in the side of his mouth. It wasn't lit, so I assumed it was there for decoration. The whole place reeked of a barnyard, or so I thought. Later I realized that it was mostly Jean-Loup.

"Well?" he said. "What is this rare gift you bring?"

"I have a business proposition for you," I said.

"You are American?"

"Yes. And like all Americans, I have money, some of which I intend to offer to you for doing a simple service."

Jean-Loup's eyes widened a little, and he smiled. Not all of his teeth were gold. Not all of them were there.

"What is it you wish me to do?"

"Simply take a car ride with me. To Tangier. And then have a talk with some friends of mine who are interested in your history."

"*My* history?"

"Yes."

125

"But why? Perhaps it is for the cinema?" He chuckled at his joke and then coughed, disgustingly. A lifetime of too many Gauloises.

"We'd like to know about the time you spent in Vichy and the way the police there interrogated you."

"Why?"

"Does it matter?"

"No, I suppose not, if you say so. But I am a busy man."

"I can see that. It will only take a few days of your time. I'm sure the prom committee can get by without you." So, too, the cockroaches. "We'll be taking a drive to Tangier, nothing more than that. And when you're finished telling us about your experiences in Vichy, we'll bring you back. There is no risk to you. None at all. There's nothing illegal about any of it."

"Really?"

I couldn't tell if he was disappointed or not.

"Really."

"How can I trust you? You may be from the Vichy yourself."

"Do I look like I'm a Vichy cop?"

"No, but appearances can be deceiving."

"True. You, for example, look like Maurice Chevalier's dance partner, but I don't really think you are."

"Bah! In the old days I could sing and dance better than that one," he said disdainfully. "He is a collaborating swine."

"So I've heard. But this little project I'm offering has nothing to do with politics. It's just that we want to understand how the Vichy police operate. That's all."

"That appears very much like politics to me."

"As you said—appearances can be deceiving."

He stroked the stubble on his chin, like a philosopher mulling over a problem. Maybe he wanted to display some reluctance as a negotiating ploy. Maybe he was doing his imitation of the crafty peasant. Maybe he was a crafty peasant. But it didn't really matter. It would come down to money. I had it; he didn't.

"Let us get down to the tacks, as you Yankees say—how much is this worth?"

"Five hundred American dollars." Why I was starting low and trying to save the Consulate's ersatz money is beyond me. The habit of frugality, I suppose.

"Truly?" He brightened up considerably. It was not surprising at all, given the condition of his den.

"Yes."

"And I would be back here in only a few days?"

"Three at the most. And we will put you up in a very nice hotel in Tangier."

"El Minzah?"

"Why not?"

"Who are the people who want to know these things?"

"My bosses."

"You are a spy?"

"No. I am the naval attaché to the American Consulate. This is a purely diplomatic mission. Some international organizations are interested in humanitarian abuses inflicted on prisoners in France. We are helping them out by gathering information."

"Like who? Which organizations?"

"The International Red Cross, for one."

"I have heard of them." He thought some more and nodded as though showing he approved of the Red Cross. "I would be willing to help them out. It is for a good cause."

"I'm glad you agree."

"But there may be a problem."

"What's that?"

"I'm not sure my papers are in order."

"We have some new ones for you."

"Really?" That apparently was welcome news. "May I see them?"

I had them in my pocket and handed them to him.

"These are very good," he said, with the eye of an accomplished user of forged documents. "But that photo does not look very much like me."

"No. It's just one we had available on short notice. It's close enough, though, don't you think?

"Perhaps. Not as handsome, though."

He grinned. It was not a pretty sight, but I was glad to see it, because I knew then that I wouldn't have to shoot him up with the dreamless. He was on board, or soon would be.

"No. Not as handsome," I said.

"Who is this Marcel Proust?"

"Just a name. A boxer from New York City."

"Ah. A boxer? Like Georges Carpentier?"

"Yes."

"Good. I like that. I always wanted to be a famous boxer, too."

"You have the face for it."

"Thank you. But I wonder why you came with these papers already prepared. You must have been very sure of yourselves."

"Not really. But we understand that we're offering you an interesting deal that will pay you handsomely for a mere car trip and a few days of meetings and discussions—all perfectly safe and legal. We figured the offer would be attractive to you, so we prepared for it. And we want to leave immediately. But . . . if you think it's too much trouble, or if your schedule is too full for the next few days, we will find someone else. There are plenty of people who've been interrogated by the Vichy police."

"That is certainly true. Then how did you select me?"

"I don't know, personally. Someone in the Consulate knew of your troubles and thought you might like to earn some money and maybe get a little satisfaction."

"Satisfaction?"

"I think you know what I mean."

"Yes. I suppose I do. Do you have the money with you?"

"Some of it. There will be a bonus for you, if all goes well and you cooperate completely."

"How much of a bonus?"

"Another five hundred."

"What if my story is not interesting to your people?"

"That's our problem. Not yours. All we want are the facts about your arrest and interrogation. Their questions and methods. That's all."

He grimaced at the memory.

"That was an unpleasant time," he said.

"I can imagine."

"I doubt it, monsieur. I doubt it. May I see the money?"

"Of course. I took out my wallet and counted out ten twenties. It made a nice little pile, and I could see the glint of avarice in his beady little eyes.

"May I keep this now? As a gesture of good faith?"

"Yes. Put it in your pocket. You'll get the remaining three hundred when we get to Tangier tonight. Then the bonus after you've met with our people. *D'accord?*"

"*Oui.* Yes. Okay."

I couldn't tell whether he believed my Red Cross story or not. I thought it was pretty good, coming as it did on the spur of the moment. I've often found it's better to concoct a lie on the spot, when you've had a chance to assess the context and characters involved. But it really didn't matter if Jean-Loup believed he would be doing good for humanity and the Red Cross. As Dave King had said, Jean-Loup believed the money, and that was enough.

I understood. I was no one to criticize. Hell, I didn't believe much of what Amanda said, but I did believe the way she slid out of her underwear, and in the moment, that was plenty. We all have our standards of belief.

"Pack your bag and come with me. There's a car waiting in the street below."

"Do I need a bag? You said I'd only be gone three days."

"Yes. But I thought you might want a change of clothes."

He shrugged. Apparently he was satisfied with what he was wearing.

Chapter Fifteen

Jean-Loup hesitated a little when he saw the trailer. The roof lifted off on a hinge for easy access. The front door was not big enough for a person to crawl through, but it was big enough for the gas cans. The hinge to the roof was cleverly hidden under the overhanging roof, so that a casual look would show only the small doorway. It was also possible to latch the roof from the inside, so that an average border guard wouldn't suspect anything if he tugged on it. And if that guard looked through the small front door, all he would see was gas cans.

When I told Jean-Loup that riding in the trailer was for his own security, and reminded him that he was traveling with forged papers, he shrugged again and climbed in behind the gas cans. He was as much concerned about his personal security as I was, and I had no doubt he had spent hours in places that were not as comfortable as this mobile doghouse. At least it was clean—far cleaner than his apartment. There was a kind of cushion and a blanket there to make a comfortable nest, and he settled in with Gallic resignation. Anticipating Jean-Loup's needs, King had also included two bottles of Algerian *vin rouge* and some Moroccan flatbread.

"I wouldn't light a Gauloises in there," I said.

"No, monsieur. I understand. Boom!"

"Ugh," said Amanda, as we drove away, after getting everyone set for the trip. "Who is that horrid little man?"

"De Gaulle's love child. We're restoring him to his rightful place in society."

"Oh, I see. Who was the mother? Bela Lugosi?"

"Greta Garbo. You'd be surprised. Without her makeup she looks very different. Unlike you, she is not nearly so beautiful in the morning."

"Thank you, darling. Well, I hope he's comfortable back there."

"Do you really?"

"Not in the least."

I might have expected her to say "Up to a point," but I knew she wasn't much of a reader, although back a few years, she'd traveled in the same crowd as the author of the line, Evelyn Waugh. They were all the Bright Young Things, so called by the London society columns.

It took us another half-hour to wend our way out of the medina and back on to the wide boulevards of the European district. And from there the road north was smooth and well-maintained. It was a beautiful day, as days there generally were, most times of the year. On our left, the Atlantic was in a good mood, and the rollers and breakers were colorful and picturesque, rather than dangerous-looking.

We passed through the village of Fedala. It was perched on the ocean side and had a small harbor. It seemed to me that the harbor might very well accommodate some good-sized ships and that the beaches around the town looked like reasonable places to land amphibious forces coming in small boats and landing craft. I didn't see any obvious defenses, although there probably were some. The French could spot a good invasion beach as well as I could.

In an hour or so we came to the city of Rabat, which was the sultan's capital. Given the delicate balance that the French—and the Spanish, for that matter—had to maintain with the sultan, the city gave less evidence of heavy-handed French officialdom. The French and Spanish had divided Morocco into two protectorates, but the sultan maintained religious and moral authority over his people and over the whole country. The Europeans needed the sultan to maintain good order, and the sultan needed the Europeans to make things run properly and to bring in and maintain the wealth of trade and other commerce. All three sat on the lid that kept Moorish resentment from bubbling over. But it was always simmering.

We drove through the city without incident and without being stopped by Vichy police, and we continued on the road north to the border of Spanish Morocco.

We drove steadily and crossed the Sebou River at Port Lyautey. I remembered Dave King's warning about not mentioning anything about the river or even saying its name, so I closed my eyes and pretended to sleep as we crossed the bridge and drove north for the next ten miles, where the road ran alongside the river. Soon the road veered back to the seacoast, and we were back in the arid land that looked like Southern California—green from plants that lived well in the semi-desert and rugged-looking mountains to the east.

We were planning to reach the border just after nightfall, and against all odds we were a little ahead of schedule. When we were well into the country, I suggested that we pull over and let everyone stretch their legs.

"I know a good spot, Lieutenant," said Moshe. "There is a grove of trees on a hill overlooking the ocean. Very pretty. It is an isolated place, just off the road, where no one will bother us. We can stop there for a picnic. Mr. King was kind enough to put together some food. It is in a hamper in the trunk."

"Sounds good. Suit you, Amanda?"

"Yes, please, God. I have to go to the loo. Are there some bushes where a girl's modesty can be protected?"

"Yes, madame. It is a private spot. I often stop there to admire the view. And to think over my sins."

"Well, I don't need to do that," she said. "But I do need a place to pee."

In another fifteen minutes we spotted the little grove of trees on the left side of the road. Moshe pulled in and parked in the shade. Through the trees we could see and hear the Atlantic surf crashing into a deserted beach. Looking around, we could see no trace or suggestion of humanity, civilized or otherwise. There weren't even any ships on the horizon.

As Moshe promised, just beyond the rim of trees there were some thick bushes, and Amanda climbed out of the backseat and hurried in that direction.

"Don't watch," she said. But she soon disappeared into the foliage.

I went around to the trailer and lifted the roof to see how Jean-Loup was doing. He was asleep, both wine bottles empty.

"No need for the sleepytime," I said to Moshe.

He said nothing, which struck me as odd, since he usually had something to say about everything and anything. But I understood why when I looked up from the trailer and saw him holding a gun—a Luger, as it happened—pointing it at me. I blurted out the obvious.

"What the hell, Moshe?"

"Not really, Lieutenant. Not Moshe. In reality, my name is Mohammed Akbar, at your service. And in the service of our friends from along the Rhine."

He smiled, I suppose because I must have looked so flabbergasted.

Despite the Luger, I was not very worried. I guess I had come to think of Moshe as harmless, and even with a gun in his hand he did not seem very menacing. His expression was almost entirely friendly. And he was relaxed. There was no suggestion of the kind of emotional volte-face a character shows in the movies when he's revealed to be the villain. No dramatic snarls or diabolical laughter.

"I thought you were a Jew—a lapsed rabbi, even."

"Yes. I know. You will remember that I told you that the Jews and Arabs were all Semites. It is not hard for one to appear like the other, especially if you have fairly light-colored skin. Many Arabs do, you know. Then all it takes is a black suit, a black fedora, and under that, a yarmulke. Throw in a few stories from Sholem Aleichem, and voilà!—Moshe Rabinowitz, the rabbi with crippling doubts and a difficult wife."

"I didn't know your last name was Rabinowitz."

"As I have just said, it isn't. Ha!"

"You got me with the dog story."

"Yes, that was a good one. I agree. That one I made up myself."

"Well, you were very convincing. Obviously."

"Thank you. Arabs do not have the same doubts about things that Jews seem to. We are not constantly feeling guilty and asking God why we have been the chosen people and could He not choose someone else for a while. No. We believe God knows what He's doing and don't question Him."

"What about the *schnorrer* jokes?"

"I had to look for those. Arabs are not besotted with irony, and there are very few Arab comedians. In fact, I can't think of any. So I had to do a little research to create Moshe. But the necessary material is readily available in a book called *The Anthology of Jewish Humor*. I thought about reading Freud's book on humor, but I figured it was a waste of time. The *Anthology* was enough."

"Did you take it from the library?"

"Ha! Very good. Yes. There was one copy in the library in Tangier. I am going to keep it, too, as a souvenir. And I'm not going to send them a check for the fines."

"Okay. So—what now?"

"Well, my people and I are very interested in your venture here with Jean-Loup. No one would take the time to extract such an otherwise unimpressive human specimen, if he did not have some unique value. We want to know what it is."

"Do you expect me to tell you?"

"No. I expect him to tell us. I don't want to hurt your feelings, but I very much doubt if you really know what's going on. At least beyond the basics. We need more than that."

"*We* being the Nazis?"

"If you like. We are in temporary partnership."

"The enemy of my enemy is my friend."

"Yes. We want the Europeans out of North Africa. And if we have to work with the other Europeans to do it, well, so be it. As I said, we are not perplexed or bewildered by irony. Or even surprised by it."

"Surely you don't trust the Germans."

"No, for the simple reason that we don't trust anyone. But we can recognize and adopt expediencies."

"If they come here, they'll never leave."

"Perhaps. But the French and Spanish *are* here now. That is a fact. The possibility of Germans is only that—a possibility. Theoretical. So what would you have us do? Nothing? If you are walking in the desert and a lion approaches you and you have no weapon other than a stone, do you tell yourself, well, it's only a stone and not likely to be effective and so I'll simply sit down and wait to be eaten? Or do you pick up the stone and do the best you can?"

"I can see your point." That was true, but it also doesn't hurt to agree with a man holding a gun, even one with a friendly look on his face.

"Of course. And suppose for a second that the Germans help us evict the French and Spanish but then go on to lose the war. That is possible, yes?"

"More than that, I would say."

"Exactly. So it is in our interest to help them in the short term."

"And then work against them later on."

"Why not? And so, it is clear to us that this adventure of yours may have some significance to the grand strategy of this war. It is also clear that this reeking Frenchman is the key to the mystery. We want to know what it is. Therefore, I am going to take the car and Jean-Loup and drive a little east to Fez and deliver him to my friends there."

"What about me . . . and Amanda?"

"Oh, well. As you see, this is a very remote spot. There is hardly any traffic along this road. I think I will just leave you both here to admire the view and wait for someone to come along. It won't take me long to disappear over the horizon, and it won't take me long to get to Fez. No more than a few hours. There is no need for violence. In our short acquaintance, I have come to like you, Lieutenant. Our cause will not suffer if you and the lady continue to live. Agreed? If I kill you both or let you live happily ever after, it will make absolutely no difference to my future, or anyone's future, for that matter. Except yours, of course. My cover will be blown either way, and I will be persona non grata, once they understand that the plan has gone awry, and I have disappeared. I can't go back to being Moshe. Nor do I want to. Moshe was a device designed to achieve a purpose. Now he is no longer needed."

Not surprisingly, I felt relieved, his friendly demeanor notwithstanding.

"Well, as someone once said, you could have fooled me."

"Yes, I think it was neatly done. Well, I think I shall be going. When the lady returns, you can explain the predicament."

Just then the lady in question emerged from the bushes. Out of the corner of my eye, I could see her stop and try to figure out what was going on. Then she reached into her purse.

"Drop it, buster," she yelled. "And don't move."

She was pointing the .38 expertly at Moshe, using two hands, arms extended and sighting down the barrel. I could see her pull back the hammer to cock the gun. She had a fierce look in her eye. She actually looked serious. Her hands were not shaking. She was only about ten feet away. Close enough, even for a snub-nosed .38.

Moshe stood still for a moment, obviously surprised by the sudden turn of events. The Greeks built much of their dramatic theory around moments like these. They called them *peripeteia*, and if Moshe didn't know the concept before, he was experiencing it now.

We three stood there for a moment or two, all frozen, not exactly like the figures on a Grecian urn, but just as immobile.

But then Moshe turned slowly to face Amanda. There was a loud bang.

Moshe stumbled backward and crumbled into the dust, his fedora blown off by the bullet hitting the bridge of his nose and coming out the back of his head, messily.

"Oh, no!" said Amanda, sincerely. "Oh, dear!"

"What the hell happened?" I said.

"It just went off. I had it cocked, and when you do that, the trigger pull gets very light."

"I know."

"I didn't mean to do it."

"I believe you."

Did I? It was an awfully accurate accident. And very convenient. In fact, it was Amanda's second convenient head shot, killing without a miss. Her husband was the first. It made a fellow think. One shot like that might be an accident, but two? And I still had my doubts about the first one.

"Is he . . . badly hurt?"

"You could say that."

"Oh, dear," she said, again. "How awful."

She came over to the body and looked down. Blood was seeping into the sandy soil. Remains of his fertile brain were scattered in the sand. "I'm terribly sorry, Moshe."

"Well, if it's any consolation to you, his name wasn't Moshe. He was a Nazi agent, an Arab masquerading as a Jewish employee of the Consulate. He was going to make off with the car and Jean-Loup and leave us stranded here. So . . . all things considered, this is not that bad of an outcome."

"Really? My goodness. An Arab Nazi agent? How very cinematic!"

"I suppose."

"So, in a sense, I have done something patriotic. Have I? I'll feel much better, if I have."

"Yes. And you didn't have to lie back, shut your eyes, and think of England."

"Don't be vulgar, darling. Poor man," she said, still looking down at Moshe. "He looks like he's smiling, though."

"Well, it may be a common effect known as rictus. But you may be right. Maybe the Muslim conception of Paradise is really true, and he's just met the reception committee of virgins."

"Yes. I've heard about that. What do women get, I wonder?"

"Handsome naval officers."

"Really? Oh, good. That seems fair." She paused as though considering something. "So Moshe was a spy. Well, well. Aren't you just a trifle chagrined at being so easily fooled?"

"Yes, I suppose so." I wasn't really, though, the more I thought about it. After all, Colonel Eddy had assigned him to me.

"You should be, darling, because sometimes you can be awfully conceited."

"Mea culpa."

"I should think so. What shall we do with the body?"

"Drag it over into the bushes and say, So long."

"Well, I don't suppose he needs a decent Christian burial, all things considered."

"No. Hardly that. Scavengers will take care of everything."

"I don't want to think about that

"Then don't. Out of curiosity, why did you take your purse with you?"

"Darling, you can't be serious. You of all people should know that we have different arrangements down there, and ladies need a little tissue for afterwards."

Well, I certainly did know that and realized my question was a dumb one. But another small part of me had to wonder. With Amanda, there was always something to wonder about. Or almost always. One thing was certain, though—she was a cool one.

Jean-Loup slept through it all. Well, a snub-nosed .38 fired in the open air doesn't make too much noise. And two full bottles of Algerian red wine will turn out the lights for most people, even experienced drinkers.

I dragged Moshe-that-was into the bushes and placed his hat over his grinning face and bid him *Shalom*. I wasn't sure that was the proper way to say "So long," but it was the only Yiddish word I knew, other than *schnorrer*. It didn't really matter, seeing as Moshe wasn't Jewish.

"Do you want his pistol?" said Amanda. "It's very handsome."

"No. You can keep it as a souvenir. I have a Luger like that from a fight in the Gulf last year."

"How dashing of you. Well, I'd better keep it. I mean, suppose we left it here, and some little child came along and started playing with it."

"Very thoughtful, Amanda. In fact, I think I noticed a school crossing just before we got here."

"You are so mean to me, darling. It's a good thing I almost love you."

"I'm glad about that. But tell me something—where did you come up with the phrase 'Drop it, Buster'?"

"I think Veronica Lake said it in one of those gangster pictures."

We got back in the car.

"You drive, darling," Amanda said. "They drive on the wrong side of the road here, and I might have an accident. Another one, I mean."

Chapter Sixteen

Fifteen minutes later on the highway north, Amanda said, "I'm starved. We forgot to have our picnic."

"True. And there's more now for us."

"You really are heartless."

"Thus speaks the pot."

We pulled over and got the hamper out of the trunk.

"Let's sit over there by those bushes. We can eat and watch the ocean."

We did. The hamper contained ham sandwiches on baguettes. There were two more bottles of Algerian red wine and some hard-boiled eggs.

"There's a cheese sandwich here, too," said Amanda. "I'll bet that was for Moshe, or whatever his name was. Poor man. He wouldn't have wanted the ham."

"Speaking of that, did you know that 'Moshe' is another way of saying 'Moses'?"

"No, of course not. Really? Aren't you clever? Well, then, Moses wasn't a Jew! How funny."

We opened the wine and poured it into the thick, unbreakable glasses that came with the hamper.

"This is quite nice," she said. "This wine, I mean. Do you like it?"

"Yes. Mixed with olive oil, it would make a good vinaigrette."

"Snob. Well, you know I don't know anything about such matters, but I do think it's very good. I like the feeling wine gives you, don't you?"

"I like the feeling drinking wine gives me, when I'm drinking it with you, my own true love."

"Oh, darling. You are such a romantic. I may fall all the way in love with you, if you're not careful."

"And who could blame you?"

When we were finished we put the hamper and its uneaten items in the backseat. We'd just started getting ready to leave when I heard some stirring around in the trailer. I went back and lifted the roof.

"Bonjour," said Jean-Loup. "I have been resting my eyes,"

"Yes. Well, it's good that you woke up because we'll be at the border soon. So if you need to get out, this would be a convenient time. After this you'll need to lock the roof and stay extremely quiet."

"Yes. I understand. Perhaps a visit to the *pissoir.*"

He got out and took a few steps, unbuttoned his fly, and let forth a mighty stream along with sighs of satisfaction, a short fart, and some throat clearing and spitting. If God had created man in His image, He probably did not have Jean-Loup in mind.

Jean-Loup finished and buttoned up. "Bon!" he said, then remembered Amanda sitting in the car. "Ah! Perhaps I should have gone farther away. I hope I did not shock the lady."

"That'll be the day. But I doubt she'll be inviting you for tea."

"*C'est la vie.* I don't like tea, anyway." He climbed back into the trailer. "I am ready, monsieur. And from here to Tangier I will be as the mouse." I heard the bolt of the lock being slid into position.

We reached the border around sundown. As we were pulling up to it, Amanda combed her hair and refreshed her lipstick and added a little scent to her wrist and neck. Not too much, though. I liked the fact that she never overdid the perfume. She was always subtle, in that way.

We pulled to the stop by the checkpoint gate. The guards were Legionnaires, both Spanish and French; there was only one border gate, and the two armies cooperated with each other and had joint custody there. There were two of them at the gate and probably a half-dozen more in the office. The two men also had a dog with them—an Alsatian. I was more worried about the dog than the soldiers.

"How romantic," said Amanda. "They look very fine in those uniforms, don't you think?"

"Yes. And this would be a good time for some sophisticated charm on your part. But don't overdo it."

She looked at me scornfully.

"Teach your granny to suck eggs," she said—a sarcastic English phrase which meant "Please don't explain the obvious to me." Apparently, all English grannies automatically know how to suck eggs. Why they would want to, though, has always puzzled me.

We opened the doors and stepped out.

"Hello, boys," she said with a dazzling smile. They both saluted, gallantly.

"Your papers, please."

I showed them my diplomatic paperwork, and they nodded and saluted me, for I was technically a superior officer.

"Thank you, sir," they said. "What is in the trailer, please?"

"Extra petrol."

They nodded and one of them opened the small front door and looked in. Then he closed it again. They spent a little more time looking at Amanda's papers while she stood there looking beautiful and perfectly at ease.

"Will you come with us, please, madame? Into the office. There is a slight irregularity, but I am sure it is nothing serious."

"Why, of course. Wait here, darling," she said to me, unnecessarily. "This won't take long."

The dog stayed behind. I began to feel extremely foolish for not considering this possibility, for the dog started sniffing around the trailer. To a dog's sophisticated sense of smell, Jean-Loup was impossible not to notice, even walled in and shielded by gas cans that also gave off a powerful odor.

I tried to pat the dog and talk to him, but he was not interested. Then I thought of the hamper in the backseat. I got out Moshe's cheese baguette and two hard-boiled eggs and offered them to the dog. He trotted over to me and sat down. He was well trained. I gave him the eggs and he gobbled them up. Then I offered him the baguette, which he took politely. He ambled over to the guard table and lay down under it to eat the sandwich.

In a few minutes Amanda emerged, still smiling, and the guards walked her to the car and opened the door.

"Thank you, madame—thank you, sir. I wish you a pleasant journey."

And we drove into Spanish Morocco.

The road was immediately worse, poorly paved and winding. But I was glad to be there.

"What was the problem?" I said.

"I don't know exactly. Something about a stamp or something. They made a telephone call to somewhere, and everything was fine after that."

It helps to be a beautiful woman. It also helps to travel with one.

"You handled that dog situation nicely," she said. "I was watching through the window, and for a minute I was a little worried."

"Dogs, cats, and babies all seem to like me."

"And who could blame them? Not me."

"Are you saying you're in love with me?"

"Desperately. But only halfway."

"In that case, maybe we should get married in Tangier," I said. "We could ask the hotel manager to perform the ceremony, just like a ship's captain. What do you say?"

"No, thank you, darling. This way is much more fun. Besides, we'd only cheat on each other, and there's a rule against that kind of thing."

"It's not a 'done' thing in your circles?"

"Oh, no, it's quite all right that way. Done all the time, of course, and no one thinks anything of it, once everyone has had a good laugh at the expense of the sinners—so shame-making for them to be caught. I just meant it's considered against the rules, biblically speaking, so there must be something wrong with it, though I can't really see what it is. I've always thought there should be only Nine Commandments. Most of my friends do, too."

"Well, forgive me for mentioning it, but weren't you and I committing something very like adultery in Hollywood, not more than a couple of years ago? I mean, you were still married to the Honorable Freddie at the time."

"Well, yes, I suppose so. But let's not talk about that now. I'm only trying to say that if you were at all reliable, and if I were at all reliable, we'd make a lovely couple. Just like the people in the *Thin Man* movies—Nick and Nora Charles and Asta, the dog. But we're not. It's too bad, really. But thank you for proposing."

"You're welcome."

"Were you serious?"

"Up to a point."

"Beast. For a moment there, my heart was all aflutter."

I was tempted to say "They can give you something for that," but her expression suggested a slight, ever so slight, suggestion of sincerity. You wouldn't think it was possible to hurt her feelings, and maybe it wasn't, but I didn't want to risk it. Every man who knew her was at least a little in love with her. I was no different.

And then a very small interior voice asked me, not for the first time, *Can you be in love with more than one woman at a time?* And another little voice answered back—also not for the first time—*Why not?*

After a fairly anxious drive on the narrow road that was pock-marked here and there with holes and cracks and frost eruptions, we finally made it into Tangier about ten o'clock that night. Not surprisingly, Amanda knew how to get to the El Minzah Hotel—the place Jean-Loup had requested. I figured we might as well humor him, until he was firmly in the grip of the OSS and on his way to London. A little extravagance meant nothing in the grand scheme of things. Besides, I figured Amanda and I deserved a little luxury, too. And whether we did or not, we were going to have it. Uncle Sam could afford it.

The hotel was in the European section of the city, of course. We drove up to the immaculately white building. The entrance was a Moorish arch that led into a huge courtyard elaborately and beautifully tiled in blue and white, with a fountain in the center and potted palms arranged along the sides. At the curb, the doorman and bellboys were dressed in white flowing robes and red fezzes. I debated putting mine on but decided not to.

The busboys took Amanda's suitcase and my duffel from the trunk, as well as the empty food hamper, and carried it into the lobby. The doorman did not bat an eye when I knocked on the roof of the trailer and Jean-Loup opened it and climbed out.

Amanda hung back a little as Jean-Loup and I walked through the courtyard to the front desk and checked in. The concierge was a European, probably Swiss, and he raised both eyebrows at the sight of Jean-Loup, but relaxed a little when I presented my diplomatic papers.

"I will need a double room for the lady and myself and a single room, next door, for monsieur," I said. "Both rooms will be on my bill and will be charged to the US Consulate. You may confirm that, of course, with Colonel Eddy at the Consulate."

"Yes, sir. Would you like rooms with a view of the harbor? They are our finest."

"That would be perfect," I said. "Okay with you, my dear?"

"Yes, please," said Amanda, demurely.

"Does . . . ah, does monsieur have any luggage?" He was looking at Jean-Loup.

"No. Not yet."

"Very good, sir." He efficiently checked us in and, with a smile of professional insincerity, gave us our keys. "The bellman will show you to your rooms, sir. I hope you enjoy your stay with us."

"Thank you. Amanda, would you please go with Monsieur Proust and the bellman? I'll be along in a minute."

"Of course, darling."

They left and I had a further word with the concierge.

"You saw the monsieur? You had a good look at him?"

"Yes, sir."

"Good. Now, would you please send someone out to buy him some suitable clothes? Suit, shirt, tie, underwear. I think his shoes will have to do."

"If you say so, sir, but his shoes—forgive me, but they were not quite—"

"I understand. But we can't be sure of the size. As for the size of the clothes, close enough will be good enough. Err on the side of too big, rather than too small."

"Yes, sir. I understand. For a moment, when you were checking in, I was wondering. He was, if you'll forgive me, sir, a trifle . . . atmospheric."

"Yes. Well, these are difficult times and call for sacrifices from all of us. Please add the cost to our room bill."

"I quite understand, sir. There are appropriate shops close by. I will have the clothes delivered in no more than two hours. Will that do?"

"Perfectly."

"I don't suppose style matters very much."

"Not at all. And basic black will do nicely."

"It might be possible to salvage the existing articles by having them laundered."

"I doubt it. They'll be better off given to the poor."

"Yes, sir." He sounded doubtful, as if to say even the poor have standards.

I gave the concierge one hundred dollars as a tip. He was pleased. I wondered once again whether it was real or fugazi—and whether it mattered. He could certainly spend it in Tangier and probably everywhere else, so was there really any difference? Another question for the philosophers.

I went up to the rooms and knocked on Jean-Loup's door. He opened it, grinning with what I took to be pleasure at having arrived in the lap of luxury. Compared to where he had come from, he certainly had. The room was beautifully furnished and opened to a balcony that overlooked the European heart of the city. Only a little way beyond that lay the modern harbor and the sea. A gentle breeze off the water was rustling the sheer drapes.

"Are you comfortable?" I said.

"*Oui.* Very. This place is *formidable.* Did I not say so? But I will be even more comfortable when I have the three hundred dollars you promised."

I reached in my pocket and showed him the bills.

"In the morning, after we have met my boss. But perhaps an additional hundred will make you sleep better."

"Ah! Yes. That would lead to the sweetness of dreams."

I gave him five twenties.

"The rest you get tomorrow. And don't forget, there's another five-hundred-dollar bonus coming."

"My memory for such things is beyond reproaches."

"I have sent out for some fresh clothes for you, Jean-Loup. We want you to look respectable when you meet our boss. The hotel will deliver them to you in a couple of hours. Compliments of the government."

"Really? Well, I suppose that is an idea with some merit. I have had good value from these I have on, but perhaps they have lived long enough."

"I also suggest that you might want to take a bath."

He looked at me dubiously, but then sniffed under his arm and shrugged.

"*Peut-être.*"

"You will want to impress my bosses—in a positive manner."

"*Oui.* I understand."

"Well, then, good night. I will call for you in the morning."

"And you will find me smelling sweeter than the gardens of Versailles. *Bonsoir*, Lieutenant."

He was a happy man.

I went to my room. Amanda was in the bathroom. I could hear her splashing in the tub.

"Is that you, darling?"

"Yes, although you must realize that anyone could truthfully answer yes to that question."

"Don't be pedantic. I am getting all fresh for you. You can join me if you like. It's a wonderful tub."

"I will, but I have to make a call first."

"Don't be too long. I don't want to get all wrinkly."

I dialed Colonel Eddy's number at his villa. He picked up on the third ring.

"This is Beau Geste," I said. "I'm here. I have Marcel Proust."

"Really? Ah, good! Well done. Let's hope Marcel still has a remembrance of things past! Ha! Is Yvonne Dubonnet also with you, by any chance?"

"Yes."

"Okay. Well, bring Monsieur Proust to the villa in the morning. Ten hundred hours. I can't talk now."

I was about to tell him about Moshe, but he hung up. He clearly did not trust the security of the phone lines. I thought he might want me to come over tonight, but I suppose he had his reasons. I was just as glad. It had been a long day.

I stripped off my clothes and went into the bathroom. Amanda was soaking full length in the tub. She had not added any bubbles, so there was nothing left to my imagination when I looked down at her with appreciation.

"Oh, how lovely, darling. You approve of what you see?"

"Yes, and then some."

"Well, come in for a minute or two, so that we can both be clean and fresh together."

I did. I sat at the other end of the tub, looking at her.

"I wonder if you'd do me a favor," I said.

"Why, darling, I fully intend to. What is it?"

"I wonder if you'd let your hair grow back to its natural color. The platinum doesn't really suit you."

"I know. It's a little trashy-looking. I thought it might be appropriate for a French chanteuse. But I'm glad you want me the way I was before. I'll grow it out just for you. Now, what else can I do for you?"

"Pass me the soap."

An hour later we were sitting on the balcony overlooking the city. The lights were shining throughout the city and on the ships in the harbor. The moon was casting a shaft of light on the surface of the sea, and the night air was cool. We had just finished room service. We had it served on the balcony, and even so, we'd eaten "starkers," because that's the way Amanda liked it. We were six floors up, so it didn't seem all that brazen to be sitting out there naked.

"Do you like the champagne, darling?"

"Yes. It's perfect."

"They had so many to choose from, I didn't know which one to get, so I asked them for a recommendation, and they said Veuve Clicquot '26."

"A good French wine," I said.

She stretched and yawned.

"Oh, pardon me. I'm getting so sleepy. I may have only enough energy to give and receive one more favor. Let's go back to bed now, darling. One more favor each, and then we'll say good night."

Which is just the way it happened.

At the end of a half-hour she looked at me with nearly closed, dreamy eyes, her face and her hair smelling of bath soap and traces of her perfume.

"That was lovely, darling," she said. "Truly. And thank you for these last few days. I shall treasure them."

"I will, too."

"Really? Promise?"

"Yes."

"I'm glad we're half in love. It makes things so much nicer than either not caring at all, or caring much too much and having all that messy emotion get in the way."

"Yes. This is much more civilized and friendly."

"That's right. That's our specialty, yours and mine. Friendly shagging."

And then I felt a sharp prick in my butt, and knew immediately that it would be eight hours before I woke up, and when I did, I would find her gone.

Chapter Seventeen

I did. And she was. And so was Jean-Loup. And the two hundred dollars in my pants pocket and five hundred from my wallet.

But she had left me a note. It was not tear-stained.

Dearest Riley,

I cannot go with you, or ever see you again, probably. You must not ask why. Just believe that I half love you, my darling and . . .

Oh, who am I kidding? I'll bet you've known all along, haven't you? The thing is, I've got a job to do, and where I'm going you can't be any part of it. I simply cannot let my lovely friends in Vichy have any more problems, and I know that you are planning something dreadful and that awful Jean-Loup is somehow part of it, so I'm taking him along on the plane to Lisbon, and from there, to Vichy. He looks and smells much better this morning, and I'm sure he'll tell us what you've asked him to do, because I also promised him the five-hundred-dollar bonus.

I borrowed the money from your pocket and wallet, because it is only fair to pay him what you promised, and besides, he wouldn't go with me without it. You will probably think that was wrong.

But you will think of me fondly, won't you? I thought it was all over between us, when I left you in Los Angeles. But it wasn't, was it? I hope none of this will damage the happy memories we have of each other. And maybe when this dreadful war is over we can meet again and resume our beautiful friendship and be half lovers again.

I hope your bottom does not hurt too much, because I never gave anyone an injection before and I may have done it badly and jabbed too hard. Please forgive me, if I did.

If it makes any difference to you, I promise to grow my hair out so it will be natural again and everything will match.

Hugs and kisses,
Amanda

Bitch!

With a sinking sensation in my gut, and an aching butt, I looked at the clock on the bedstand. Nine o'clock.

I called down to the concierge and asked what time the plane for Lisbon left. *Eight o'clock.* Was it likely to have been delayed? *No. The weather was good and the plane had left on time.* What time did the lady and the fragrant gentleman leave? *Around six-thirty.* Plenty of time to get to the airport. How did they get there? *Taxi. No luggage.* No luggage? *No, sir.*

I hung up and looked in the closet. Amanda's suitcase was still in there.

I took it out and opened it. It was almost empty. No wonder it was so light when we left Casablanca. There was only a slip of hotel stationery. *We'll always have Casablanca.* And under that she had placed a lipstick kiss. The only other thing was my .38.

Well, if she needed a gun, she had Moshe's Luger.

Bitch!

It was almost time to meet Eddy at his villa, so I dressed in my uniform. Maybe that would remind him that I was really just an active-duty officer and not a professional spy, and therefore might possibly be forgiven for what could only be called an epic fuck-up and disastrous breach of security for Operation Torch.

True, Dave King had said it was okay for me to give Amanda a ride—that she was harmless—but I was still in charge of the job. I could have said no. I knew damned well why I'd wanted to bring her along. So if Colonel Eddy and the rest of them wanted to say I had been led astray by a devious femme fatale and should have known better, well, they'd have every right to say it, and more.

I went downstairs to get a taxi, but it was not necessary. Seaman Davis was there in the jeep, waiting for me.

"Good morning, sir," he said. "Have a good trip?"

"Mixed," I said, glumly.

Colonel Eddy was on the patio when we drove up. He was smiling broadly.

I figured that wouldn't last.

We sat at the patio table and the steward brought coffee.

"Well, sir," he said genially. "How was your trip?"

So I told him about losing Jean-Loup, about Amanda and about Moshe—the whole stinking mess, from start to finish. His expression didn't change during my *auto-da-fé*. He was calm and didn't interrupt or ask questions.

"So that's it," I said, miserably. "I can't tell you how foolish and inept this whole thing has made me feel."

"That's understandable," said Eddy. Then he smiled. "But you shouldn't be too hard on yourself, because the truth is, things worked out exactly as they were intended to."

"What?!"

"Well, maybe not exactly. But close."

"What do you mean?"

"Think back on the orders Dave King gave you in Casablanca. What did he say that you must never repeat to anyone?"

"The words *Port Lyautey* and *Sebou River*."

"Right. That's because our friend Jean-Loup never was and never will be a river pilot on the Sebou. He was, however, an experienced river pilot on the Rhône River, in France. When Amanda delivers him to the Vichy authorities, which also means German intelligence, they will question him and learn that we more or less kidnapped him, and they will assume it's because he knows the Rhône. What will they deduce from that?"

"That an invasion is planned for Southern France."

"Yes. We're not ready to go into Europe yet. Realistically, we might not be ready until 1944. The Germans may or may not know that, but they do know there's clamoring for a second front, and that we've got to do something, somewhere, and pretty damned quick, if only for political reasons. They know we'll be coming, most likely sooner rather than later, but they don't know where. If they learn from Jean-Loup that the Rhône area is the likely target, so much the better.

"As for Torch, if the Vichy think we're going into Southern France, that will increase our element of surprise when we hit Morocco and Algeria, which is defended by Vichy troops and their navy. Do you remember that story I told you about floating a body ashore with phony papers? Same idea."

"So Jean-Loup is an unwitting plant?"

"Yes, and all the more believable for that. It's called disinformation in the trade. He can't tell them anything he doesn't believe. He's the best kind of double agent, because he's not aware he is one."

"What about Moshe?"

"Well, we were on to him. That was another reason not to mention the Sebou."

"Really? How did you get on to him? He sure as hell fooled me with his Yiddish act."

"You're a Presbyterian from Ohio. Perhaps you missed certain subtleties."

"True. But I also worked in Hollywood. I'm no stranger to all things Yiddish."

"I guess you're right. The fact is, I only got wise to him by accident. He didn't know that I grew up in this part of the world, and I recognized that his occasional use of an Arabic word was perfect, but his Hebrew and Yiddish were sometimes incorrect. There was no way to check on his biography, of course, but it was soon pretty clear he was an Arab agent, and like a lot of these dissident Arabs, he was in bed with the Germans. We made sure by sending a few phony stories through him. Trifling little things designed get a reaction from the Gestapo here, and when they did react, we knew Moshe had passed the information to them."

"So he was supposed to kidnap Jean-Loup."

"That was the original plan, yes. But when Amanda came along, Dave King figured that she would give us a useful fallback in case something went wrong with Moshe. She's been working for Vichy from the start of the war."

"But Dave King said she was okay."

"Yes, well, he *would* say that, wouldn't he? She gave us backup in case something happened with Moshe."

"Like what?"

"Who knows? Moshe could have easily been arrested by the Vichy police. They might have had a dossier on him as an Arab dissident. They're not completely asleep at the switch, you know."

"That's possible, I guess. He did tend to sweat a lot at police checkpoints."

"For good reason. Besides, we were aware of your history with Amanda and figured it could somehow work to our advantage."

"You got that from Bunny."

"Yes."

"Was that the reason I was recruited for this job?"

"It's possible, I suppose. One of them, anyway."

"What about the Sebou River? Was that all BS?"

"Oh, no. Not at all. It's still very much in the plans of the brass in London and Washington. We still want to take the airport at Port Lyautey, and we still want to use the river to do it, if at all possible. And we still need good information about its navigation. The idea of grabbing a river pilot is still a good one. In fact, it was the original idea. This whole other plot involving Jean-Loup and disinformation came afterwards. Sort of a flash of inspiration."

"So I suppose I'm being sent back to Casablanca to do it all over again and transport the real guy."

"No. It's already been done. There's a man called René Malev-ergne who has worked on the Sebou as a pilot for years. Knows every inch and mood. And last year he was arrested by Vichy and held in prison for several months. It soured him on them completely. He was released and came back and got a job in a cannery in Casa-blanca. He quit the river but knows all there is to know about it. So we approached him, and he agreed to work for us. One of our agents drove him up to Tangier last night and put him on a Royal Navy ship to Gibraltar about an hour ago."

"Drove him up here in a trailer?"

"Yes, as a matter of fact. He'll be on his way to London later today, and from there, on to Washington. He'll meet with the staff planning the Casablanca operation."

"Then what the hell was I supposed to be doing?" I knew the answer, but asked anyway.

"You were a decoy. Just in case the Vichy or the Germans got wind of the idea somehow. That's why you left first—before the car with the real pilot."

"I see. The cheese in the trap."

"If you like. But think of it as a very good kind of cheese. In the end, you had two functions, decoy and disinformation—either one of which was vitally important, but in combination, well, we'd call that a home run. You'll get a medal out of this. I'll see to it."

"Even though I had no idea what I was doing?"

"How many heroes know what they're doing while they're doing it?"

And how many of de Gaulle's two hundred and forty-six kinds of cheese know they're cheese?

"There's more good news," said Eddy. "The repairs to your ship are under way. She's been moved into a dry dock. Chances are very good she'll be ready for the actual Torch invasion. I can't tell you when it will be—I don't know. But I can guess it will be toward the end of autumn. Plenty of time for your ship to be put back together and made ready. So you'll be able to come back to the scenes of the crime. Fun, eh?"

"When do I get my orders to return? I assume you only needed me for this one job."

"Yes, because you were unknown to all the bad guys and very well known to one rather naughty girl. Now you're blown, as they say, so it will be on to something new. As for your orders, I have them here." He tapped his coat pocket, exactly the way Bunny had done not so long ago. "The boys in London would like you to stop by on your way and give them a debriefing on the mission. I don't suppose you'll mind that, eh?"

"No, sir."

"And Riley, although you may not appreciate it now, you did a really good job on this mission. As you boys in the navy say—well done."

"Thank you, Colonel. But maybe you will answer me one question."

"If I can."

"Suppose Amanda had not come along and it was just me and Moshe and Jean-Loup. Moshe told me he didn't see any reason to shoot me and leave me along the road, but what if he hadn't felt that way? I would've been in a tight spot."

"Yes, that's why you'll get a medal. But we didn't figure Moshe for a killer. There was really no need for it, from his point of view. Despite what novelists might think, it's not that easy to shoot someone in cold blood, especially when there's no need to do it. But this is war, and we had to be willing to take that chance. Either way, though, you would have achieved the result we wanted."

"Good to know."

"But we're much happier it worked out the way it did. Much. You may rest assured that we considered that angle, when we decided to let Amanda go along. We figured she'd reduce the risk. Shooting two people in cold blood is more than twice as hard as shooting one, especially when one is a beautiful woman. Some Arabs have a refined sense of chivalry. Their literature on the subject is very interesting. We just didn't figure on her shooting Moshe."

"That would have ruined everything, if she hadn't been an agent."

"Yes. But she was. And we knew it."

Yes, and they also knew something else—if Moshe had shot both of us, the whole disinformation scheme would *still* have worked out the way King and Eddy had wanted it to. And what's more, Moshe would have eliminated a beautiful and presumably useful Vichy spy. A nice, neat alternative scenario. And of course, because of the way it actually did work out, the Germans were now short one spy—a phony rabbi with a fund of *schnorrer* jokes.

Either way, King and Eddy figured to win. My friend Tony the Snail Scungilli, who ran a gambling ship off of Los Angeles, had never had a better hedge.

"She says it was an accident," I said.

"Do you believe her?"

"Amanda? Who knows?"

"It's certainly possible that it was, and that her accident saved your bacon," said Eddy. "After all, we don't really know what Moshe was going to do. He may have been saying one thing and planning another. Not likely, maybe, but if I were you, I'd think of it that way."

"When I see her I'll say thanks—just before I strangle her."

"That would be a shame. I don't think you were really in too much danger from either of them. Besides, you were armed. We knew about your experience with the cops and criminals in LA, so we were pretty sure you'd make out okay in a showdown with Moshe. And Amanda may well be useful to us again sometime. She's an opportunist, not an ideologue. You must have enjoyed your time with her."

"Yes, as a matter of fact, I did. We'll always have . . . something, I guess."

Eh?"

"Nothing. Just a figure of speech. What would have happened if neither Moshe nor Amanda grabbed Jean-Loup—for whatever reason?"

"That would have been too bad, but not a disaster. Remember, your first duty was as a decoy. That worked. The real Sebou pilot is safely on the way to Gibraltar, so, primary mission accomplished. We would have found some other way to get Jean-Loup into Vichy or Gestapo hands. There are plenty of their agents around. Worst case, we could have paid him to defect."

"Oh." I paused. "One last thing."

"What's that?"

"Did Dave King mention something to the Valkyrie about Amanda? Did he set that up?"

"I don't know. But you know, Amanda's not the only opportunist in our little game. Anyone who's capable of inventing exploding mule shit is capable of just about anything. Dave enjoys his work. He smiles a lot. Maybe you noticed."

"I guess I did. Still, it would be nice to know."

"Words to live by. Are you familiar with Keats?"

"A little."

"Did you ever run across his idea of negative capability?"

"I don't think so."

"He said negative capability is 'when man is capable of being in uncertainties, mysteries, doubts, without any irritable reaching after fact and reason.' It should be the motto of our business."

"When ignorance is bliss, 'tis folly to be wise?"

"Ha! Good one. But, no. Not quite the same idea. Same church, different hymn."

Chapter Eighteen

That afternoon I went to the Consulate and met with the bean counters. I turned over the balance of the ten thousand, and they were perfectly satisfied with my accounting—three hundred advanced to Jean-Loup, seven hundred stolen from my pants pocket and wallet, and a hundred to the hotel concierge, listed as a bribe. That was it. They were so easy about the whole thing that I half regretted not padding my expenses a little. I would have felt a bit guilty about doing it, but it would have been the kind of guilt I could live with. Besides, the money was probably fugazi. As it turned out, I could leave Tangier with a clear conscience, at least as far as money was concerned.

Also at the Consulate was some mail for me. It had come via diplomatic pouch, forwarded by the Fleet Post Office. There was a postcard with a picture of the El Floridita Bar in Havana, and on the back, she'd written:

> *I'm home, temporarily. I'm hoping for a new assignment.*
> *Maybe it will be somewhere near where you are.*
> *Write and let me know things.*
> *M.*

Well, there were certainly some "things" that were better left unspoken and unwritten about. But Martha understood the boundaries of wartime security and censorship, so she was probably just asking whether it might be possible to meet somewhere in the future.

Frankly, I had no idea, but I was glad to hear from her. I'd write to her when I got back to London. This latest business with Amanda hadn't affected my feelings for Martha in any way. Should they have? I was probably not the one to ask. Worrying about how I *should* feel never keeps me awake; worrying about how I *do* feel is what does it, sometimes.

The other was a letter from my friend, Hobey Baker, the pen name of a writer who was toiling in Hollywood's movie factory.

Greetings, Old Sport,

How are things with my friend, the modern Hornblower? Speaking of that, did I tell you that the bird who wrote the Hornblower books has just skipped town because of an impending paternity suit? Well, he's a Brit, so he has someplace to escape to. Lucky lad. The lady in question is described as a fading opera singer. Ouch. These newspaper boys can be so insensitive.

My life has been looking up ever so slightly. I got a job doing some script doctoring on a movie they're just about finishing up— rather a soppy melodrama, set in your current part of the world. Bogart is in it. He's the romantic hero. Can you believe that? Was no one else available? Was Ralph Bellamy too busy?

Funny thing is, they're still not sure how it's supposed to end, even though principal photography is supposed to wrap in a few days. There's this triangle and no one knows quite yet who's going to wind up with the girl. People are frantically writing tomorrow's scenes the night before. My job is to clean up some of the remaining dialogue, which will require some minor re-shoots. There's one line that shows you the extent of the soppiness: When the hero takes a glass of champagne, he looks at the girl and says "Here's mud in your eye." I mean, really!

I'm supposed to come up with something better than that. Well, I can do that in my sleep. Even "Bottom's up!" would be better, but that might not get by the censors, who, as everyone knows, have dirty minds and see double entendres even when they weren't intended.

They haven't asked me yet how to fix the ending of the picture, but it's clear to me what should happen—Bogart gets the girl, and fade out. The other character in the triangle is an oh-so-earnest European stiff that no girl in her right mind would prefer even to a sad sack like Bogart.

On the other hand, in real life she's about six inches taller than Bogart, which means he has to stand on a box during the love scenes, and it's a good laugh when they're supposed to be dancing together. They just have to stand there swaying back and forth because Bogart can't maneuver very far standing on an overturned case of Pabst Blue Ribbon.

Bogart's sidekick in all of this is a Negro piano player played by a Negro who can't play the piano and has to fake it. I'm not sure that he isn't actually a white guy from Oslo. Nothing else is real. Why should he be?

My other career as a writer of scripts for those ten-minute travelogues is also looking up. Did I say "also"? Well, looking up. I came up with an idea that the studios love—instead of sending a second-rate camera crew to these various appalling places, why not use stock footage from old movies that have been shot, distributed, and forgotten? I mean, a deserted beach with waves crashing into a jungle could be anywhere. You just have to say that it's Mozambique or Tierra del Fuego, and voilà, it is! And the street scenes with happy natives could be anywhere there's photogenic poverty and slums and farm animals lying in mud puddles.

It's a brilliant idea—use existing pictures, re-edit them, and simply write a new narration. The studios love it because they can get some unexpected mileage out of old film, and there are no travel or crew expenses and no problems with the Reds in the union.

Because of this, they've made me executive producer of a new venture called Worldwide Travel Films, Inc. I'll travel the world without leaving LA County. Was it Thoreau who said "I have travelled a good deal in Concord"? Well, I'll be doing something similar. And I write better than he did. (But most people do.)

I'm going to do the next one on Bolivia, and I hope that there is a beach there somewhere. If not, I'll show one anyway. We have too much good stuff on beaches. And who's going to know the difference? Out in Peoria they don't know Bolivia from Bacteria. With luck, Bolivia has some Indians down there, too. We have some good outtakes of extras standing around looking picturesque from the last Hopalong Cassidy picture.

All of the gang here at the Garden of Allah send their best wishes and hope that you are not getting shot at or bombed. We are all getting bombed nightly, but that's nothing new.

All the best,
Hobey

Typical Hobey. The Garden of Allah was a hotel on Sunset Boulevard where he and I and a bunch of transient writers and actors lived. It was an adult frat house. Those were the days, and in Hobey's case, they still are.

But his letter got me thinking about Hollywood, which, as most people know, is a con factory with palm trees. All surface unreality. Like they say about the Platte River—a mile wide and an inch deep. But it made me wonder—how different was it from this business I had just finished? In a lot of ways—not much. Not much.

Then it suddenly occurred to me to wonder if maybe, just maybe, Amanda was a double agent. Maybe she was really working for us. After all, on the phone Eddy had seemed ever so slightly surprised when I'd mentioned I'd made it here with Jean-Loup. And then he asked if Yvonne, meaning Amanda, was with me. He didn't seem to want me to bring Jean-Loup to his villa that night, even though it would have been much more secure there than at the hotel. That seemed a little odd, now that I thought about it.

After Amanda gave me the shot in the butt, she'd had plenty of time to call Eddy and ask him what he wanted her to do. And this morning, when I'd half seriously suggested strangling her, he had said she might become useful in some way. Was it possible she already *was* being useful—that maybe delivering Jean-Loup to the enemy was not only giving them a dose of disinformation, but also inserting her into their intelligence circles—demonstrating her worth as a valuable agent to them? Jean-Loup was her pass, her ante, her bona fides to the Germans. Maybe that had been the plan all along, the plan concocted by Eddy and Dave King and Amanda together.

But wouldn't the Germans wonder why she had shot their man Moshe? Yes. Probably. But maybe her story was going to be that she was working for Vichy and didn't know Moshe was working for the Germans. It wouldn't be the first time different spy agencies hadn't talked, especially different agencies from different countries, and one of them, Vichy, being a reluctant partner, at best. She could say she thought Moshe was what he appeared to be—a loyal employee of the Americans, helping them kidnap a valuable intelligence asset—Jean-Loup. So shooting Moshe really *was* a kind of accident—even if she had intended to do it. That would be an appropriate level of irony.

The more I thought about it, the more it seemed simpler and safer just to say that I had shot Moshe, when he'd threatened us. Who was going to contradict her?

All of which led me to the next question—as a former girlfriend once said, when I told her I was joining the navy—"What about me?" Frankly, the question had confused me, and I had no answer.

Same now. Why did Eddy and the rest leave me so completely out of the loop? Why not tell me what Amanda was doing? What Moshe was doing? Why leave me so completely in the dark?

On the other hand, from Eddy's point of view, the real question was, why tell me anything? After all, there was no benefit to my knowing, and lots of possible downsides from my unintentionally giving the game away—to Moshe, even to Jean-Loup. Why bother? Why risk it?

There wasn't all that much risk. But there was no reward at all. No point. Hell, I wasn't even in the loop about being a decoy. I'd been in the navy long enough by now to understand the concept of "need to know." And on this assignment I hadn't really needed to know anything. I was just a wedge of cheese—albeit robust and smooth, with perhaps a suggestion of sophistication.

Then I thought—if Amanda really was a double, she was going into the lion's den armed only with her looks and charm and her talent for fake insouciance. Could she really be that brave? Sure. Knowing her, sure. And could she pull it off? That was a different question. But I liked her chances. Hollywood actresses had nothing on her.

So I decided that if I ever saw Amanda again, I would not strangle her. I felt better about the whole thing, even if this interpretation of events was nothing more than my own invention, like Hobey's beach in Bolivia. I could think of her fondly by telling myself she was really on our side all along . . . maybe.

I'd see what Bunny had to say about it when I got to London. Maybe he'd tell me the truth. But he probably wouldn't. Why would he start now? Besides, maybe not knowing would be better for my peace of mind. That way I'd always have fond memories of Amanda. That way we always *would* have the good times.

The situation reminded me of my time as a PI in Los Angeles. The LA cops were always talking about some places in the city where they never could, and never would, know what was really going on. One of those places was Chinatown. Well, this place was like that. In Morocco, it seemed you could never be sure of the score, or even who was playing. Was it therefore a metaphor for something larger? Was being here an exercise in Keats's negative capability?

These were all questions better answered by philosophers, poets, and script writers. I could live with not knowing, and even without knowing whether any of it mattered.

So I decided to stop thinking about it.

I had said good-bye to Colonel Eddy after our meeting, and I had my orders to return to London "soonest." From there I assumed they'd send me to my ship at the Clyde River shipyard outside of Glasgow.

It would be good to get back to the simpler pleasures and duties of a naval officer. At least in that job you knew who your friends were and who the bad guys were, and you knew what you were supposed to do and something about how to do it, and the explosions came from bombs and artillery shells, not phony mule shit.

I had an afternoon flight to Lisbon. And from there, on to London.

I took off my uniform and changed into my diplomat's white suit and dark tie. I packed up my stuff and headed for the airport, wearing my fez. Not quite a dunce cap. Not quite.

THE END